In the Stars

In the Stars

STACIA DEUTSCH AND
RHODY COHON

Simon Pulse
New York London Toronto Sydney

This book is a work of fiction. Any references to historical events, real people, or real locales are used fictitiously. Other names, characters, places, and incidents are the product of the author's imagination, and any resemblance to actual events or locales or persons, living or dead, is entirely coincidental.

〰

SIMON PULSE
An imprint of Simon & Schuster Children's Publishing Division
1230 Avenue of the Americas, New York, NY 10020
Copyright © 2007 by Stacia Deutsch and Rhody Cohon
All rights reserved, including the right of reproduction in whole or in part in any form.
SIMON PULSE and colophon are registered trademarks of Simon & Schuster, Inc.
Designed by Ann Zeak
The text of this book was set in Garamond 3.
Manufactured in the United States of America
First Simon Pulse edition August 2007
10 9 8 7 6 5 4
Library of Congress Control Number 2007922439
ISBN-13: 978-1-4169-4875-9
ISBN-10: 1-4169-4875-9

To my family.
With love, Stacia

For Tiffanie Bialis, chemist and
woman extraordinaire, and Alzada Tipton,
friend and devoted reader.
Cheers, Rhody

One

The planets are aligned in your favor.
It's time to start something new.
www.astrology4stars.com

I've lost my mother's diamond. Not the whole ring, mind you, just the diamond.

Cherise says it's a sign.

"A sign of what?" I ask.

"A sign of your future." There's a gleam in her dark brown eyes. "It's a sign that true love is coming your way."

"Yeah, right," I snort. Not a ha-ha funny snort, but a full throttle, you-are-out-of-your-mind kind of snort. "You crack me up."

Cherise snorts back at me. Only louder and better. Her snort actually echoes off the walls of the school hallway, bouncing from locker to locker until some freshman girls at the end of the hall turn to see what the racket's all about. They glance nervously in our direction then rush off to class.

We look at each other and both start laughing. It's absolutely hysterical that the girls ran off. If they'd just hung out a little longer, they would have discovered that Cherise is not the type to harm the young. Quite the opposite in fact. She's all about love and peace and cosmic harmony. Cherise was born in the wrong decade. She should have been a flower child of the sixties.

Cherise Gregory has been my best friend since kindergarten, and lives in the apartment above mine. When she's not attending rallies for gender equality or animal rights, Cherise's favorite pastime is finding signs in the universe and interpreting their meaning.

You might wonder why Cherise and I are friends at all. I like factual, hard science and keeping my feet grounded in the reality of what's happening today, not what might be someday. While Cherise lives for tomorrow and side-trips into metaphysical fantasy.

We may seem entirely different on the

surface, but once you get to know us, you'll see that Cherise and I have lots of things in common. And for those things we don't have in common, well, that's what makes our friendship interesting.

I've always thought that we're good together because we balance each other out. We both love hangin' at the Corner Café (it's like our home away from home), reading romance novels (Cherise takes them seriously, I just think they're fun), watching classic movies (we especially like the ones with happy endings), and of course— looking up at the stars. We are both really into the stars. The big dif is that we come at our passion for the nighttime sky from different perspectives: Cherise is into hoo-ha voodoo astrology, whereas I prefer the academic pursuit of astronomy.

Don't get me wrong, I'm really supportive when Cherise uses astrology to forecast the weather, intuit what questions will be on our exams, or make personal decisions like if she should buy the black or the brown clogs. On the flip side, she's infinitely patient when I regale her with some little-known fact about the molecular makeup of Saturn's rings or feel the burning need to share pictures of the Eagle Nebula. We each have our own perspective on the stars and we're fine with our differences. I would even say it enhances our friendship . . . most of the time.

I've never tried to press Cherise to take a more scholarly approach to the planetary system and only once before has Cherise ever dared to make a prediction about anything connected to my personal life. It was seven years ago, and neither of us have ever mentioned it since. That's why it's incredibly odd that today she's interpreting the loss of my mother's diamond as something more than what it is: the accidental loss of a valuable, sentimental stone.

"It's definitely a cosmic marker," Cherise reiterates as I grab my books for class and a bottle of water from my locker before flinging it shut. The doorjamb is bent. I have to slam the door over and over again to finally get it closed.

"I don't really see how losing the diamond out of my mother's ring can be a signal of impending romance," I say as I twist the combination lock, mixing up the numbers. "Really, Cherise, you sound like a bad fortune cookie."

"You know I'm right." Cherise's locker

is next to mine. The door closes smoothly. It clicks shut, but Cherise doesn't twist the lock. She leaves it unlocked, preferring to trust in the goodness of human nature instead. So far, no one has stolen from her.

"Sylvie, you aren't in tune with the universe," Cherise tsks, while we head down the hall toward the one class we take together, English Literature. "Good thing for you, I am." She grins. "It's so obvious. Diamonds are the stone of engagement. Engagement is what inevitably happens to a couple in love. When you find the right guy, he'll give you a diamond of your very own." She seems quite sure of herself. "Losing your mother's diamond means that the right guy is coming soon. Really, really soon." Cherise smiles widely. Her straight teeth are a reminder of the years we suffered through braces together. "I have no doubt. Love is headed your way, Sylvie Townsend."

As usual, Cherise's logic is beyond comprehension. It's a pretty big leap from losing a diamond to falling in love. It reminds me of the time in junior high when she got the stomach flu and interpreted it to mean that a big blizzard was coming. Don't ask how she made that connection. I have no idea either, but the snow started the next morning and school was closed for a week while the city's maintenance crew shoveled out the town.

As much as I like to tell myself that Cherise's predictions are ridiculous, things generally seem to happen the way she says they will. Weird, but true. As a scientist, however, I will tell you there's no possible way she has an inside track on the universe, so let's just say that what Cherise calls "predictions," I call lucky guesses. And in general, Cherise is an exceptional guesser.

But not this time! This time, Cherise has got it all wrong.

"You're nuts," I tell her. "Love is not headed my way. I don't want to find the right guy. Or even the wrong one, for that matter. No guys at all. And I definitely don't want a new diamond." I'm speaking in a strong voice, so that there can be no misunderstanding. My tone softens when I add, "I just want to find my mom's."

Losing the stone reopened the pain I felt at the time of Mom's death. In those days around her funeral, I felt lost and empty inside. Like someone had kicked me so hard the wind went out of my chest. It took me months before I could set one foot in front of the other and move forward, literally. That diamond was my physical link to her. And now . . . it's gone.

When I went to take a shower early this morning, I noticed the stone was missing. I don't know if I lost it yesterday, last night, or this morning. My head hurts from trying to recall the last time I saw it glimmering in its white-gold setting.

In the little time I had before I rushed off to school, I tore apart the living room. Next, I skipped breakfast with my father, choosing to scour my room instead. Then, I scrubbed the kitchen floor, mopped the bathroom, and checked the tub and sink drains. I even stopped at my father's tuxedo shop to look around.

It's nowhere. Gone.

"That diamond reminded me of *her*," I say with a sigh.

We reach our classroom and pull off to the side to let other students enter.

"You don't need a ring to remember your mom." Cherise reaches in her purse and pulls out her herb-infused, 100 percent organic, paraben-free, pressed-powder compact. "You have her face, her hair, and her eyes." She opens the lid and rotates the small reflecting glass toward me. "You can remember her just by looking in the mirror."

What she's saying cheers me up a bit because I know it's true. I have blue eyes, straight, honey-colored hair, and a light smattering of freckles across the bridge of my nose. It isn't just my face that looks like Miriam Louise Townsend: I'm thin, flat-chested, and a full head taller than many of the guys at school. All traits inherited from Mom. Sometimes I wonder if my father contributed any of his genes at all.

Cherise turns the mirror back toward her, powders her nose, then shuts the compact with a snap. "Now, Sylvie," she says as she stashes her makeup back in her bag, "since love is headed your way, I think we should talk about your outfit."

"You're offering fashion advice?" I reply, taking a second to survey Cherise's gauzy get-up. Her broomstick skirt with appliquéd flowers came from a retail store that guarantees the cotton was organically grown, without pesticides. Her teal-colored hand-embroidered blouse came from another place that certifies that no child labor was used in manufacturing. Her sandals are hemp, since wearing leather would be cruel to cows. Socially conscious retail comes with a socially conscious price tag. Luckily, Cherise's parents support her causes.

I look down at my faded jeans, Keds, and well-worn tank top. I think it used to be orange, but now it's a soft brownish color. I almost always have a sweatshirt tied around my waist in case it gets chilly. So what? I like comfy clothes. Besides, Dad and I are always struggling to make ends meet, so I don't have a lot of extra money to spend on the latest fashions. Usually, I get my stuff at the thrift shop in Clifton Heights.

Cherise's style suits her, and my style suits me.

"No way we're talking about my outfit," I tell her. "I look fine."

"*Fine* is passé," Cherise responds. "You're going to want to look *glam* for your new love." She begins to describe a faux fur jacket she found online, which she thinks I'd look good in.

I smooth out a wrinkle in my tank top. "I don't need new clothes. I'm not falling in love." I put up a hand to stop her from interrupting. "To fall in love, first I'd have to go on a date," I say firmly. "C'mon, you know I don't date. I need to keep my head down and my grades up until my academic future is secure. That's all."

It's not that I couldn't get a date if I wanted to. I mean, I probably could. I'm not a total waste. I'm smart and funny and when I want to get dressed up I turn out better than some other girls I know. Plus, as far as I can tell, flirting isn't as hard as determining whether Pluto is a planet or an asteroid.

It's just that I don't encourage any of the guys at school. To be completely honest, I do what I can to keep them from approaching me in "that" way. Cherise says I send off neg vibes. I don't know if it's vibes or not, but it works. Besides, our school isn't that big. It's in an older, settled, part of Cincinnati. Cherise and I have known the same guys since elementary school. The dating pool is more like a toddler's plastic wader.

So it's perfect grades. Perfect school attendance. Perfect behavior in school and out. That way, nothing is going to distract me from my goal.

I want to be an astronomer like my mom was. This is my senior year of high school, and I desperately hope to win a scholarship to Yale University (my mom's alma mater).

I've already been accepted to the school, but I can't go without a full ride. They only give five science-based scholarships away every year and I'm solidly in the running. My entire being is focused on that scholarship.

Only eight more weeks until graduation. I've already submitted all the proper paperwork. It's a waiting game from here, but I am not going to do anything to mess this one up. A slight dip in my GPA, and Yale will become a distant memory.

Maybe, before I leave for Connecticut, I'll consider a light summer romance, if I can find the right guy, but not now. Not today. No way. And for sure, I'm not going to fall head-over-heels in romance-novel love.

Since I started high school, I've been watching the girls around me drop like flies. Their brains turn to mush as boys smile at them in the lunchroom and say "Hey" in the hallway. I see the girls I went to junior high with (girls who I thought were bright and clever) suddenly wasting hours at the mall, buying makeup and miniskirts. Instant Messaging instead of doing homework! Even texting boys during class. From there it's a slippery slope to study sessions with no studying, late-night parties, and dropping grades. I even know one girl who got pregnant!

Funny, isn't it? While every other girl I know is trying to get a date, I'm trying to avoid one. I stay away from trouble. No weekend parties, no drinking, no boys, and just one friend, who doesn't date either, though her decision is by choice, not necessity. Cherise simply isn't interested in dating. She uses every free second she has to volunteer and "save" something.

I turn toward Cherise. She has an omniscient look in her eye, a glowing scrutiny that indicates she knows what I'm thinking. I bet she practices that look in the mirror at night because it's really good. It just doesn't have any effect on me.

"I'm not interested in love," I say. "I don't have time."

"I *knew* you'd say that." Cherise raises one eyebrow. "But the cosmos have suddenly shifted. You can wear your secondhand clothes and send off your leave-me-alone vibes, but no amount of repellant is going to change your destiny. You'd better get used to the idea, Sylvie. Love is headed your way."

I open my mouth to protest. Cherise

flashes me a sideways glance and, oddly, my brain doesn't connect with my mouth.

Grinning wildly, Cherise opens the door to our classroom and holds it for me. As I walk through, she says, "I'm going to come visit you at work after school. Losing that diamond is the biggest cosmic indicator I've personally ever encountered! I need to draw up your astrological chart." And with that she heads inside, ready to study English.

I can't seem to form a coherent argument against her wasting my time with silly astrology.

The diamond isn't the only thing I've lost.

It seems I've lost my mind as well.

Two

*Your typically dead-on intuition
may be faulty right now, especially
in dealing with a special person.*
www.astrology4stars.com

The school day's over and, as usual, I'm sitting in my comfy chair at the back of my father's tuxedo shop, hemming pants.

After school and on weekends, I work in the shop. Today is Monday, so here I am. Of course, if it were any other day, I'd be here, too. I haven't missed a day of work in seven years. Really. I've never taken a sick or "personal" day. I went away for one week two years ago, but my father closed the shop and took a short break himself while I was gone, so that doesn't count.

I've helped out around here off and on since I was a kid. After Mom died, it just seemed natural that I'd do as much as I could. When I was younger, I would sweep up and match cummerbunds with bow ties. Now I'm old enough to be a seamstress and desk clerk. Every afternoon I sit in an over-stuffed chair in the back of the office, adjusting black tuxedo pants with a needle and thread. I know hand-sewing is old-fashioned. Sewing with a machine is more fun, but when it comes to hemming, I like the precision I can get with a plain ol' needle.

Hemming is methodical and soothing. It takes my mind off the imminent arrival of Cherise and her astrological charts. I've excellent reason to be wary. When she originally bought her planet-plotting software seven years ago, I was her first reading. Being a good friend, I agreed to let her make my chart. I told her the time of my birth and then promptly forgot about the astrological nonsense. A few hours later, Cherise knocked on my door with tears in her eyes.

She had bad news: Someone I loved was going to die. Two weeks later, my mother was diagnosed with cancer. Not even six months afterward, she passed away.

I don't believe that there was even the slightest possibility that Cherise might have had advanced notice of my mother's illness from some ridiculous planetary chart. And I don't, for one second, think that Cherise could have possibly known Mom was going to die. The planets just don't work *that* way.

I never told Cherise to keep her other astrological predictions away from me. I didn't have to. She's my best friend. In the last seven years, Cherise has never mentioned anything about the sun sign of Virgo again. As I told you, she has kept her predictions to blizzards, test scores, and the occasional celebrity breakup—that kind of stuff.

Until today.

Needless to say, I'm not looking forward to Cherise bringing my chart to the shop this afternoon.

I cringe when front door chime rings.

I hear my father's voice from the register. "Sylvie, your friends are here."

Friends? I wonder as I tie off my sewing and tuck the needle into a pin cushion. I have one friend. Not *friends*.

I peek out to the front room before stepping into view. Sigh. Two girls in my graduating class, Jennifer Riley and Tanisha Merston, are standing near the window display looking at a wedding gown.

Last year, my father mentioned that a wedding dress in the window would be a great marketing device to bring engaged guys and their groomsmen through our door. We couldn't afford to buy one, so I decided to take a stab at making the dress. My father bought me the fabric and a pattern.

I think the dress turned out really great for my first try. Normal people start making clothing with less ambitious projects than a wedding dress, but I'm an overachiever. I didn't even really follow the pattern. I made lots of changes along the way. I added more lace to the bodice and gave the gown a shorter train. The dress turned out just the way I imagined it and I loved creating something so beautiful.

Jennifer and Tanisha are still looking at the gown. I can hear them talking about who they'd like to marry, what they'd wear, and generally dreaming about the ceremony.

Wedding gowns do that to girls. A nice-looking wedding dress can take any college-bound high school student and turn her into a love-lost giggling girl ready to chuck her education for a fine-looking man and a big diamond ring. Any high school girl, that is, except me. And Cherise.

When the girls are done looking at the gown, they turn toward me. Time for some niceties.

"Jennifer," I greet her, stepping lightly into the room. I'm consciously trying not to drag my feet like I do when I'm faced with a task I'd rather avoid. Jennifer has blond hair piled high on her head and the most perfect nose of any girl in the whole school. Maybe even the whole city. I wonder if it's her original nose.

Tanisha isn't so bad either. Her jet-black hair falls in carefully coifed ringlets around her face. Her eyes are dark as midnight, and her skin is smooth. Rumor is that Jennifer and Tanisha want to work in the fashion industry after high school and I have no doubt they will. They're both super fashion-able already. I nod toward Tanisha and say simply, "Hi."

The thing is, I don't really hate Jennifer and Tanisha. I just don't have anything to say to them. These girls represent popularity, boys, and cheerleading. I represent academic overachievers, girls without boyfriends, and students with jobs. We're polar opposites. We're so entirely and completely different that girls like Jennifer and Tanisha usually make me feel awkward and uncomfortable.

I will admit though, of all the "popular" girls at school, Jennifer and Tanisha are the only ones who are always nice to me. It's not like they invite me to sit with them at lunch or anything like that, but they make a point to smile and wave in the hall.

The question is: What are they doing here? They've never been to the tuxedo shop before. They must want something.

"Hi, Sylvie," Jennifer says. "How are you?" I want to reply with a noncommittal, "Fine," and get back to work, but something in her tone makes me think she really wants to know.

"Okay," I say. And then tack on, "I've been really busy lately, doing homework and stuff." Deep breath and then reciprocate. "How about you?" I hope I sound equally sincere.

"Good," Jennifer replies. Tanisha adds in her bubbly way, "Terrific."

"Is that your dad?" Tanisha asks.

I glance over my shoulder at my father. He hasn't said anything, but he's looking at the girls with interest. The only person who ever visits me in the shop is Cherise. I'm sure his curiosity is brimming over. Not that he'd ever ask me to introduce them or anything like that.

My father and I don't talk much. He was way older than Mom when they got married and I'm not convinced he ever really wanted children. I've always thought that I must have been a surprise. A happy surprise for my mom, which was just hunky-dory with him—as long as he didn't have to raise me. Which, in the ironic way of the world, he did. It's not that I don't love my father. I do. I'm certain he loves me, too. But we really don't connect or have much to say to each other. Just the facts. And an introduction to Tanisha and Jennifer, well, that just isn't the kind of fact he needs.

Besides, they aren't going to be here long enough to leave footprints in the carpet. After I find out what they want, I'll hustle them out the door.

My father runs a hand through his salt-and-pepper hair and pushes up his wire-framed glasses. He's always dressed to the nines at work; not in a tux, but in a dark suit with a patterned tie. He must have a zillion different ties. I doubt he's ever thrown one out. I know it seems odd that he dresses so nicely and I prefer the thrift-shop look, but he doesn't spend a lot of money on his clothes. He mostly makes them himself, if you can believe that. Even the ties.

Between regular work and sewing after hours, you'd expect that my father lives in the tuxedo shop, but he somehow seems to have enough hours in the day to read the paper and watch the evening news, too. I wish I was heir to his time management skills. I always have to plan things much more diligently.

Right now, he's looking at Jennifer and Tanisha as if he expects me to introduce them, but I'm not going to. To my relief, the phone rings and my father turns away to answer it.

"Well, I bet you're wondering why we're here." Jennifer tosses her head, and not a single hair comes loose or even wiggles.

Tanisha steps up to the plate. "You know, the Spring Fling Prom's coming up soon." I nod, unsure where this is heading.

"We're going with our boyfriends," Jennifer says, as if the whole school didn't know they both had boyfriends.

Tanisha again. "Jennifer and I heard that you're an amazing seamstress." She gives one of those girly giggles I could happily live without ever hearing again.

I knew they wanted something. Should I remind them that one wedding dress does not make me either amazing or an actual seamstress?

"I—I—I—," I stammer, ready to make excuses.

Jennifer raises one hand to stop my protest. "This year, the dance is a costume ball." She pauses for dramatic effect. "Tanisha and I thought that maybe you'd help us make our costumes. We designed them ourselves, but we've got a problem. Neither of us knows how to sew." She reaches into her bag and pulls out some drawings.

I'm suddenly having arm spasms. I find my hands acting on their own to take the sketches.

There are three drawings. The first is a wood nymph, complete with wings. The skirt is comprised of small silvery whispers of fabric, which float around the nymph's legs.

Wings rise from the costume's back, in sheer mesh and gauze. This is out of my league.

The second is an Old English gown of gold lace and russet velvet. I can see the hint of a cotton under-dress. Way, way out of my league.

If the first two drawings were good, the third is spectacular. It is obviously a fairy-tale Cinderella princess. But not a Disney costume. More modern. Less flashy. Exactly what you'd imagine a common girl who marries a prince would feel most comfortable in. Blue and yellow and simply cut. It is a dressmaker's dream.

But I am not a dressmaker. I might have made one, but with the single exception of the wedding dress, I'm simply a tuxedo hemmer. And a maxed-out student focused on a full scholarship to a highly competitive school at that.

"I can't do it. Sorry." I thrust the drawings back to Jennifer. "I don't have the time. And I'm not really interested in the Spring Fling dance."

"I told you—," Tanisha begins to complain to Jennifer, but Jennifer silences her with a look.

"Keep the drawings." Jennifer hands the

papers back to me. "There's a whole month before the dance. Plenty of time to make the dresses. Plus, we'd never ask you to do all this work alone. Tanisha and I will be your apprentices."

At that, Tanisha smiles a big fake smile. "We'll do anything and everything you ask."

"And we'll pay you," Jennifer adds.

I desperately want to ask, "How much?" because I could use the extra cash for college. Yale is far away, and expensive. The scholarship will cover most of my expenses, but that doesn't stop my father, in his own cautiously supportive way, from dropping the name of the closest in-state university, where I could live at home and keep working in the shop.

If I stayed in Cincinnati, I'd go crazy. I need to get out. It's time for me to find my own place in the world. And the tuxedo shop is definitely not my place. My dreams are waiting at Yale and once I snag that scholarship, I could really use some extra cash to help pay for books and food. Maybe even a new telescope.

Hmmm. I know that even asking Jennifer and Tanisha how much they might give me would be foolish since I don't want the temptation. "I just can't," I say as the door chime rings again.

Cherise comes in, humming a tune of disjointed notes and clashing melody. She's carrying her school backpack made of recycled tires, casually slung over one shoulder.

I notice Jennifer and Tanisha huddle together. I totally understand their reaction to Cherise. Earlier this year, Tanisha showed up at school carrying a Gucci purse trimmed with fox fur. Animal-loving Cherise went ballistic. She didn't dump paint on Tanisha's purse like some freaked-out activist, but the next morning Tanisha arrived at school to find her locker had been covered with PETA stickers and posters of baby foxes looking out with big sad eyes from wire cages. The posters were stuck to the metal with some kind of mega-glue that took weeks for Tanisha to remove (the janitor told her it was her locker, therefore her responsibility). Of course there was never any "proof" that Cherise was the vandal, but both Tanisha and Jennifer have kept their distance ever since. (And, no surprise, Tanisha has never shown up at school with *that* purse again.)

They move as a unit past Cherise toward the door. "Think about it," Jennifer says as she opens the door. "I'm the wood nymph. Tanisha is Guinevere. Cinderella's yours." The bell chimes again as the door slams shut.

"What was that all about?" Cherise asks.

"Nothing." I reach around my father, who's still on the phone, and stuff the dress drawings behind the counter. "They wanted to talk about the Spring Fling Prom."

"Hmmm," Cherise squints her eyes suspiciously. "First the diamond, then the Fashionistas talking to you about the dance. Definitely another cosmic marker. Things are lining up perfectly." She raises her eyebrows to appear more all-knowing (I've seen that look a thousand times), but it doesn't work. She comes across as crazy.

"Not a cosmic marker," I retort. "A project that I don't have time for."

My father announces that he has to run over to a hotel to pick up some rentals that had been left there by a careless group of frat boys. That leaves Cherise and me manning the shop.

"Fate is hard at work today," she announces, following me as I retreat to the rear of the shop and settle back into my chair. "We've been left alone. Time to get to business."

I pick up the trousers I've been working

on. "I *am* doing business." I wave the pants in front of her. "I can't fool around, Cherise. I need to finish these up and then review my calculus notes for tomorrow's quiz."

"You do your business"—Cherise smiles a wicked grin as she drags a chair next to me and sets up a small folding table that was stashed in the corner—"I'll do mine." She sets the table between us.

Since the Jennifer/Tanisha thing took up some of my precious time, I figure I might as well let Cherise get on with her show. The faster she reviews my astrological chart, the faster she'll leave. I start sewing, but at the same time I'm biting my tongue and hanging on for the ride.

"Your birthday is September 22nd," she tells me as if I didn't already know. "And you were born at 9:12 in the morning." She must have remembered that information from the reading she made all those years ago. "Just like your DNA, your astrological chart hasn't changed since your birth."

I yawn. Totally intentionally. If she thinks I'm tired, maybe she'll cut me a break and leave.

My plan fails. Cherise settles in, then reaches into her backpack and takes out a large piece of white paper. On it, she has drawn a big circle, carefully divided into twelve pizza sections. Numbers one through twelve label each slice. She has written notes all over the paper.

"You are a Virgo with Libra Ascendant," she informs me. "In fact, based on your birth date, you ride the Virgo/Libra cusp."

Very interesting. (I'm kidding. It's not.)

"This isn't a solar chart, it's a natal one," Cherise tells me as she whips out a pen and uses it as a pointer. "You share a solar chart with everyone who was born on the same day as you. Because I am using your birth time along with the date, this natal chart will be far more accurate."

During the two seconds I actually pay attention to Cherise's explanation, I accidentally poke myself with the needle. It hurts, but luckily, doesn't bleed. I'd hate to have to explain to my father why I bled on these pants. I am going to have to ignore Cherise better and concentrate harder on my sewing.

"Your moon is in Libra," she explains, pointing at a pizza slice she referred to as "First House." "This means that you want to be appreciated for your hard work. You'd like to accomplish something that will make you famous." She is staring hard at the chart, trying to decipher her own handwriting. "You're disciplined and curious. Driven and focused."

At this I have about a million snappy retorts, the first one being, "Duh. You could have known those things by hanging out with me since kindergarten." Instead, I look at my sewing and count stitches as she talks.

"You're also moody and oversensitive." Again I'm biting my tongue not to say, "Duh." Then she adds, "You have a romantic edge, but it's mostly manifested through the books you choose and the movies you like to watch." I think she's at "Duh!" times three.

Cherise skips ahead to the "all-important Seventh House," the House of Relationship. "Saturn sits in Capricorn," she excitedly tells me, as if this is the news I have been waiting my whole life to hear. "It means you're cautious about romantic liaisons. You don't want to get involved until you're certain that not only the man is right, but that the timing's perfect." At this she smiles, turning the chart toward me. "And here's the good news: The timing is now and the guy is on his way!"

I look down at her drawn circle, her chicken-scratch writing, and shake my head. Gibberish. I'm looking at a page full of nonsense.

"Do you mind if I light a few candles?" Cherise pulls two out of her school bag—a blue one she insists is for her own spiritual clarity and a red one to bring me love.

"Not a chance," I reply. "In the name of our longtime friendship, I'm letting you spin your astrological mumbo about me, but even the best friendships have limits. I can't risk you burning down my father's shop."

Cherise sets the candles out anyway, but doesn't light them. They're so heavily perfumed I think I'm going to suffocate from the overwhelming mix of vanilla and cinnamon.

Cherise turns the chart back toward her and stares at it.

Then she does some strange witchy wiggle with her arms. Apparently I'm not the only one with arm spasms today. When she's done shimmying, Cherise proclaims, "Mars is entering Gemini. Love will take over where logic once governed. Your heart will soon be bonded to another." She sighs the dreamy sigh of a teenaged girl on the brink. "Love is in the air, Sylvie. It's written in the stars."

Yeah, yeah, yeah. "All right, I've heard enough," I insist, pausing my hemming long enough to let her know exactly what I think. "You've been lucky with your guesses before, but not this time," I tell her. "I study astronomy. The stars don't have the power to forecast the future. Mars is simply traveling on the same elliptical orbit it has always traveled on. Astrology is not a science. Astronomy is." I am on a roll. "There's no data or objective observation proving that astrology reveals anything about us as individuals or how our lives will progress."

I'm about to boot Cherise out of the shop, in the loving way friends tell each other to go away, when I notice she's running her finger over one part of the chart and humming. It's not a joyful hum, but a hum of wonder and amazement. A hum designed to attract my attention. Clearly she ignored my whole astronomy/astrology lecture.

"What?!" I feel a rush of annoyance, oddly mixed with curiosity.

"Wednesday," she recites slowly, the word rising to my ears on a whisper.

"What about Wednesday?" I ask. Because I'm supposed to, not because I want to.

Cherise lowers her head so that I can no longer see her eyes and says in a slightly spooky voice, "Mars enters Gemini on Wednesday. Wednesday is your special day. The day your soul mate will be revealed and—"

"We're done here," I quickly cut her off. I put down my sewing and gather up her chart. "Time for you to go." Cherise tries to block me, insisting that she isn't finished yet, but I'm too quick. I hand her the paper and, in one swift move, fold up the table.

While she's packing up her backpack, Cherise tells me, "I'll check out your daily horoscope in the morning."

"Whatever," I mutter, giving in to the fact that there's no stopping her. I'm headed to the front of the shop, hoping Cherise will take the clue and follow me. She follows, but slowly, almost haltingly, as if she is enjoying my discomfort.

Cherise finally opens the door to let herself out. "Oh." She turns back toward me. "You should wear gray. That's Virgo's special color. I have a new gray-striped skirt that was made by blind nuns in Guatemala. You could wear it Wednesday . . ."

I adore Cherise, but I'm done with her for today. "Out!" I charge.

Later, well after I put her astrological reading out of my mind and return to my hemming, I notice that Cherise secretly slipped the red candle of love into my purse.

Three

You are at a loss as to how to proceed
with an attractive person. Loosen up
and start the conversation.
www.astrology4stars.com

Wednesday has arrived. I am *not* wearing gray. In fact, I've taken great pains to make certain there is no gray anywhere in my outfit. I even left my watch at home on account of its gray woven band. I'm not going to get sucked into Cherise's nonsense.

Cherise called last night to tell me she'd left me a surprise package outside my apartment door. It was the gray skirt she wanted me to borrow. Very cute, but there was no chance in hell that I was going to wear it.

Not today. Not ever. I have to give it back to her. Immediately. Unfortunately, Cherise has an early class on Wednesdays, so I'm not going to see her until lunch. I can't leave the skirt in her locker on account of her keeping it unlocked all day. So I have the skirt in my backpack, with the hope that I can catch her in the hall between classes.

When I get to school, it's a convenient surprise to find Cherise's twin brother, Tyler, hanging out in the hall near my locker. Cherise and Tyler might be twins, but they dress like night and day. Literally. Where Cherise wears brightly colored flowing gauzy free-range frocks, Tyler dresses completely Goth. He wears black. Nothing but black.

From his shoes to his pants to his belt to his shirt—if I turned off the lights, Tyler would disappear. His too-long hair is dyed the color of midnight. Tyler wears it slicked back in a small ponytail and then ties a black bandanna around his forehead.

I have to admit, I do get a kick out of the fact that he wears the earring I gave him last Christmas at their family's Christmas gift exchange. My father keeps the tuxedo shop open late Christmas Eve for formal-wear emergencies, so I usually spend the evening with Cherise's clan. After seven years, it's become a tradition.

Tyler's earring was meant to be a joke—a skull and crossbones to go with his all-black pirate motif. The joke didn't go as I expected. He's worn the earring every day since.

Without taking the time to find out what he wants, I shove Cherise's skirt at him, telling him to return it to her, that I don't even want to be near the thing.

Tyler takes the skirt from me and agrees to give it to his sister when he sees her next period.

I like Tyler well enough but ironically, given the amount of time I spend with his sister and family, I don't really know him very well. In all our years, I swear I've never actually had a full-fledged conversation with him about anything. Tyler's a bit like furniture that happens to be in the room. If you're sitting on the sofa, do you really notice the end table? My friendship's with Cherise. Tyler's a lot like her shadow—he even dresses the part.

This is why I'm so surprised when he asks: "Want to grab a bite after school today?"

"Huh?" His question throws me off for a second. Cherise and I regularly "grab a bite" at the Corner Café after school, before I head over to the tuxedo shop. Tyler simply shows up, nearly every day, whether we've invited him or not. No one has ever made plans to go to the Café . . . we just go and have been doing it for years.

I know, being as busy and scholarship focused as I am, it's hard to imagine that I waste time over a piece of pie every single day. But I do. I'm most comfortable when I have a routine. I like unwinding from school before I have to go to work. And the pie at the Corner Café is to die for!

"Want to go to the Corner Café?" Tyler asks, as if we might be going somewhere else. Is there anywhere else?

"I'll be there," I tell him, unclear why we are having this conversation at all.

When Tyler opens his mouth again, as if he has something more to say, I worry that he's going to hand me back the skirt. I don't want to give Tyler the chance to turn down my errand, so I interrupt whatever he's about to say by telling him I'm in a rush and then hurrying down the hall.

Three class periods later, I'm entering the chemistry laboratory. After this, there's lunch, and then two more classes. In another thirteen hours, it will be Thursday. I will have survived Wednesday and Mars will be moving out of Gemini, for whatever that's worth. (Not that I've given Cherise's prediction a second thought or anything.) At precisely midnight tonight, I will have made it through the day without discovering my "soul mate." Ha-ha-ha.

At the stroke of midnight, I'm planning to call Cherise and tell her exactly where she can stick her astrological chart.

Hang on a second! Someone's sitting on my chem lab stool!

It's my stool because that's where I always sit. *Always.*

I look at the already-filled room and survey the laboratory tables. Yep, that's my table, third from the right, under the window. My table and my stool. Everyone knows it. So why is someone sitting there?

Ever since Showgo Yakimora moved back to Japan in the middle of last semester, I've had my own setup in the chem lab. I like it that way. Being the only one without a lab partner, I rely solely on myself to make sure experiments are done properly. I've worked extra hard to be a standout in chemistry lab. Chemistry is an integral part of astronomy. It's all about how molecules move and combine to form special matter. No dumb dude who's happy with a passing C in chemistry just to graduate high school is going to ruin my course grade.

I mix my own chemicals, monitor my own outcomes, and never, ever, ever, share. Mistakes are my mistakes and the joys of discovery are all mine, too.

So what is some brown-haired, green-eyed, good-looking guy with nicely cut arm muscles doing on my stool at my lab space?! And why did I notice the color of his eyes?

Something bad is happening, and I don't have to be in tune with the universe to know it.

"Sylvie," Mrs. Wachmeister reprimands me from the front of the room. "Why aren't you sitting down? We are about to begin."

"I know," I start, "but—"

"No excuses, young lady." She uses her long pointing stick to indicate an empty stool at the back of the room. "Bring that stool over and sit next to Adam Forrester." She moves her pointer to the interloper sitting at my table. "I've already introduced him to the class. His family just moved to town from California. He'll be your new lab partner."

Any words after his name are completely

redundant. I can see for myself that he's a new student. And I can surmise, by the fact that he's invading my space and touching my equipment, that he's going to be my lab partner. I feel a stabbing pain well up behind my eyes as I march to the back of the room to haul the stool over to the table. *My* table.

Taking deep, calming breaths, I drag the stool across the room. It makes a sharp, scraping sound that seems to soothe my nerves.

As I pass Phillipa Goetz, she touches my back and mutters, "You go, girl!" to me. From another table, Madeline Reinhart whispers, "Lucky!" from behind her thick glasses. I've no idea what they are talking about. Getting a new lab partner is a stroke of terrible misfortune, not good luck.

After taking my time to position the stool at an angle to the table, I step up on my tiptoes and settle down onto the seat. Unfortunately, one stool leg is shorter than the others, and the stool wobbles left. Unable to react fast enough, I tip over, nearly tumbling into Adam's lap. He grabs my arm to help me steady myself.

If I had to take an oath, I'd swear he held onto my arm for at least ten—if not fifteen—minutes before I was able to redistribute my weight and precariously balance back on the broken stool. In reality, he probably only touched me for a few seconds.

"Careful," Adam says, releasing me. I can still feel the warm place on my arm where he held me steady. "I guess this explains why that stool was in the back corner over there."

As Adam speaks, he tosses his head toward the back of the room, but I don't follow his eyes. I physically can't. I'm staring at him as if he has two heads. My eyes won't move. There's no connection between them and my brain. My heart's racing and I keep staring at Adam for no apparent reason.

When my brain finally reconnects, I understand why Phillipa cheered me on and Madeline called me lucky. If you put aside the fact that he's encroaching on my turf, you'd discover the simple reality that there's a new guy in town and he's a babe. Up close, his eyes are even greener than when I first saw them from across the room. It's hard not to stare into them. A girl could get seriously lost in those eyes.

The lab begins, and, after muttering "thanks" to Adam for catching me, I force myself to pin my own eyes on Mrs. Wachmeister.

Since our high school doesn't offer

astronomy, except as an after-school club, chemistry's my favorite subject, and maintaining my A+ average is essential to snagging that college scholarship. With that in mind, I close off my surroundings and focus every fiber of my being on Mrs. Wachmeister giving the daily instructions:

"In this experiment, two separate and distinct chemical reactions will be created through the use of an aqueous solution from three different compounds. Changes during each reaction will be obvious. You will note your observations in your notebook, due to me at the end of the period."

Happiness, pure and simple. I feel like myself again. Mrs. Wachmeister is speaking my language. Adam? Adam, who?

Mrs. Wachmeister goes to the blackboard and writes down two balanced chemical equations for the reactions. I diligently copy the equations into my notebook:

$$Na_2CO_3(aq) + CaCl_2(aq) = 2NaCl(aq) + CaCO_3(s)$$
$$CaCO_3(s) + H_2SO_4(aq) = CaSO_4(s) + H_2O + CO_2(g)$$

I wish everything in the universe could be as straightforward as the easy-to-understand law of conservation of mass.

Since Adam is new, I volunteer to gather our equipment. Two balance corks, an Erlenmeyer flask, a rubber stopper, a graduated cylinder, and two test tubes. I grab my goggles and my coat, then walk to the storage closet at the back of the room to find safety wear for Adam. I do it, but I'm not happy about it.

I hand a coat and goggles to Adam. With their scratched white plastic cover, the goggles cover his eyes, which is good for me because his eyes seem to hinder my ability to function normally.

He measures the sodium carbonate solution and pours it into the Erlenmeyer flask. I stopper the flask. And to my amazement, everything goes great. In fact, the rest of the lab time passes in a blur.

While we're working Adam says, "So I hear you're the top student in chem class."

First I blush, embarrassed that he's heard anything at all. Then I tighten my lips, hoping that he isn't planning to ride my coattails for an easy A.

"I asked around before class began. Gotta know who the competition is." He winks one gorgeous eye. "I like to have a dedicated lab partner. Not some dope who just needs a C to pass. I need to do well in chemistry since I'm going to be a doctor—a pediatrician. I'm going back to California for school. I've already been admitted to UCLA to study pre-med." Adam smiles at me. He's not conceited, like you might think a pre-med guy would be. He's . . . well, he's nice. Very nice.

I have to admit I was wrong at first about him. Looks can be deceiving (especially really good looks with well-defined arm muscles.) Adam's not some dumb athlete, come to mooch off my GPA.

Before I respond to his academic challenge, Adam says, "Forget the competition stuff. I don't want to have an academic battle with you. As long as we are lab partners, we can be a team."

"All right," I agree. "We can share the top honor." Being tied really won't affect my scholarship, as long as my grades don't slip. And I can immediately tell, with Adam at my side, the scholarship will remain in the bag!

We're working together on the experiment when Adam asks me, "Is there an astronomy club at this school? I didn't see one posted on the club board."

Did I just hear what I thought I heard?

We get to talking and it turns out he's almost as interested in the stars as I am. Adam isn't planning on a career in astronomy, but was the treasurer of his old school's astronomy club and would love to stay involved. He used to camp a lot with his folks when he was a kid and one night realized he wanted to know more about the stars. He's been learning about them ever since.

I know what you're thinking: Here's a cute guy who just happens to get placed at my chem lab table. He's an academic over-achiever, like me. Enjoys astronomy, like me. Also happens to be an only child, like me (he told me while we mixed the solution). And it's Wednesday.

All coincidence. Really. Adam was supposed to start school on Monday, but had a cold and his mom suggested he wait until he felt better. He tried to take the first-period chemistry class, but had to change his schedule to fit in AP art history. That, and his parents weren't even supposed to move to Cincinnati. Until last month, they thought they were headed to Allentown, Pennsylvania, instead. See? Total coincidence.

Plus, the probability that we are destined for love, after having known each other for, I check my watch, forty-three minutes, is next to nil.

As class comes to an end, I have to say it was weird sharing my learning environment with another person, but as I got to know Adam better, it wasn't nearly as uncomfortable as I imagined. He was really meticulous about measurements and even offered to wash the beakers once we're finished. I, of course, let him. Damn, if you're forced to have a lab partner, he might as well do the cleaning up part, right?

When Adam returns from the sink, where he's carefully rinsed and dried our equipment, he calls me by name for the first time. "I'm sorry, Sylvie," he says, "I don't know where everything goes. Would you mind showing me?"

I can't really say no since I was the one who got the stuff. Besides, this means he can gather the equipment tomorrow.

He hands me the test tubes first. They're warm and still a little damp. I grasp them in my hand and reach for the Erlenmeyer flask. Like a DVD running in slow motion, I see him hand me the flask, I feel the wetness, and realize it's too slick to hold. I watch, detached from my body, as the flask slips out of my hand and crashes to the floor.

There's glass everywhere and I'm horrified. I've never broken anything in chem lab before—not that it will affect my grade or anything that traumatic—but I pride myself on a clean record. A record that, with the fall of the Erlenmeyer flask, has just been shattered.

Mrs. Wachmeister, though alerted to the crashing noise, has made it clear in the past that the lab team is responsible for the cleanup.

Adam bends down to retrieve some of the bigger pieces of glass. "No big deal. These things happen." And then he apologizes for not drying the flask more carefully.

I immediately squat down to help him clean up the mess I made. Adam asks me to move my leg so he can get a piece near my left foot. When I do, he gasps. Next thing I know, he's swept me off my feet and is holding me firmly against his hard, sculpted chest.

I know all the science-focused guys at our school and can safely say that not one of them has a chest like Adam's. I know flab when I see it. Adam, from what I can tell, has none.

"Mrs. Wachmeister," Adam calls over his shoulder as he carries me toward the door. "When the flask broke, Sylvie was hurt. May I have permission to take her to the nurse's office?"

"I'm not hurt," I insist as Mrs. Wachmeister comes to where Adam has stopped, near the exit. "Or maybe I am," I say as I look at the fresh red blood covering my ankle and dripping onto my white tennis shoe. Once I've noticed the blood, the pain begins in earnest. I grimace.

Mrs. Wachmeister pulls some paper towels from the holder near the sink and after careful inspection presses them to the base of my ankle. "Go on." Mrs. Wachmeister gives me a sympathetic look. "I'll take care of the mess. Tell Nurse Frankel that he should look for glass fragments." And with that, she wraps my ankle in a temporary bandage and then turns away to clean up my broken flask.

"Adam, you can put me down now." We're at the end of the hall. Classes are going to be letting out for lunch soon and students will be filling the hallway. No matter how much pain I'm in, the last thing I need is for the entire student body to see Adam carrying me around. "I can walk."

"No chance." He pulls me even tighter against his chest. "You're hurt, and I'm taking you to the nurse."

Arguing seems pointless. Even though I could walk if he'd let me, I give in. I settle back and try *not* to enjoy the ride. I refuse to think about how nice it feels to be held by him, or how good his neck smells. I will not lose focus. I begin a mental mantra that goes, "Yale scholarship. Yale scholarship. Yale—" Shoot. So much for absolute concentration. I can't help but notice we are headed the wrong direction.

"Adam," I say, "This is the long way to the nurse's office. If we cut through the lunchroom, we can get there a lot faster."

Adam turns us around. "Are you suggesting I'm not strong enough to carry you the extra distance?" Even as he asks the question, he's heading into the lunchroom.

Like the teenager I am, but desperately try to suppress, I blush.

"I didn't mean to imply—" Just then, my cell phone rings. Well, it doesn't *ring*, it vibrates. I can feel the awkward shivering movement somewhere between my butt and Adam's arm. I wish I'd left the phone in my locker instead of stuffing it in my back pocket. This is really embarrassing on so many levels.

Shifting slightly left, I feebly attempt to get to my right back pocket. The movement squashes me even more tightly against Adam and, horrified, I pull away.

My sudden pullback causes Adam to stumble. He lurches forward, still cradling me in his arms, attempting to regain his balance.

It's a tense few seconds, but he manages to find his feet and settle me back in his arms.

The phone keeps buzzing. "I'll just ignore it," I tell him.

"Hang on." Adam stops walking. In one fluid motion, he shifts me up and toward him and somehow manages to support me so I can reach into my pocket to get the phone. He's even stronger than I imagined. Sigh.

I get the phone and we are on our way again. The ringing of the phone actually helped me to relax. Now I've something to think about other than the way Adam is holding me or which of my body parts are touching which parts of his.

I open the phone. It's not a call after all. It's a text message.

"After all that, I hope it's important," Adam comments as we hurry through the lunch room.

"Huh?" I'm still staring at the message on the small cell screen.

"An emergency?" Adam repeats.

"No." I quickly shut the phone cover and close my fist around the phone. I wrap my arm around Adam's neck, not so much to enjoy the few seconds I have left in his arms, but rather to keep from falling. At least that's what I tell myself.

"Anyone important?" Adam is digging for info, but I can't possibly explain to him what I read.

"Just my father," I tell Adam, a bit too smoothly. "He wanted to make sure I was available for dinner."

Adam nods. He must know I'm lying. Only the coolest dads know how to text message. But what else can I say? I can't possibly tell him the truth.

The message is from Cherise:

Mars has entered Gemini.
Phase one is now complete.

Phase one?!!!!

Four

Pairing off seems to be the pursuit du jour,
but you are not inclined in that direction.
Be your own person and enjoy!
www.astrology4stars.com

I'm at home with my foot propped up on a pillow. The phone is ringing and I have to stretch across my bed and roll on my side to answer it. Man, that hurt. I have seven stitches right above my ankle. I watched the ER doc sew it up. Working in the tuxedo shop has made me an expert on sewing stitches. Looking at the ones on my ankle, I would have made the sutures a bit tighter and finished differently, but all in all, I'd give the doc a high grade.

He sent me home with crutches. The doctor said that by tomorrow the swelling will start to go down, so I'll only need them for a few days.

I grab the phone off the handset and resettle myself on the bed before answering. I figure it's Cherise calling to tell me how her "prediction" is coming true. I'll say, "Lucky guess." She'll say, "Astrology isn't about luck. It's about *knowing*." We'll go back and forth like that for a while until we agree to disagree and move on to a more important topic, like the way our English teacher spits when he speaks.

I don't even bother to look at the caller ID. I push "talk" and say, "Hey Cherise."

It's not Cherise.

"Hello." "Hello." Two voices at once. I can immediately tell that Tanisha and Jennifer are sharing a cell phone. They must have their heads together and are both trying to listen and talk at the same time. "Sylvie?" That one is Jennifer. "How are you?" asks Tanisha.

Do I really have to answer that? I'm injured. It's painful.

"Fine," I lie. "Just fine."

"Does it hurt?" Jennifer asks.

"A little," I mumble through clenched teeth, wondering where my father put the prescription painkillers.

"Well, you're missing all the fun here," Tanisha says.

"Hmmm," I reply, not committing to the conversation. I find the bottle and pop one in my mouth. I chase it with a sip of water.

"Everyone's talking about how gallant Adam is. The way he carried you through the school." Jennifer sighs heavily. "They're calling him Prince Charming." She finishes with another romantic sigh.

"We dubbed him PC," Tanisha adds. "And your PC's the most popular boy at school right now. Gavin Masterson says he's a shoo-in for the swim team."

There's a sickening feeling in the pit of my stomach, and not because of the painkiller I just swallowed. Gavin Masterson is captain of the swim team and I dislike him intensely. I'm still bitter about all those times that Gavin swiped Cherise's lunch money when we were in fourth grade.

For all her peace-loving, save-the-world stuff, I know for a fact that the one person Cherise can't stand is Gavin Masterson. She dodges him in the hallway, averting her gaze, but I see the fire underneath. It's been eight years, and we both still think Gavin is pond scum. I should warn Adam to keep his distance.

"Does Adam even swim competitively?" I wonder aloud. That would explain his chest and arm muscles, not that I'm still thinking about them or anything like that.

"He's on his way to try out for the team this afternoon," Tanisha explains. "Word is that he swam at his last high school. He's even trained with some college guys and their Olympic coach! Now he wants to swim for us."

An image of Adam in a Speedo flashes through my brain. I bite my lip to dispel the vision and better concentrate on what Jennifer is saying. I swear I taste blood. "Just think about it," she rambles on, "you could wear the Cinderella design and Adam could dress like PC. I'm going to e-mail you the name of a costume shop that rents prince costumes. You can forward the name to him. It'll be terrific."

"What?" I missed something.

"You're going to go to the Spring Fling Prom with Adam, aren't you?" Tanisha asks in all seriousness.

My head is spinning, and I can't be sure if it's the painkillers or the conversation. "I just met him. I don't know him. He hasn't asked. I don't want to go to the Spring Fling—"

"We gotta run," Jennifer says, totally ignoring me. I can hear the school bell in the background. "Can't be late to class. Bye."

"Feel better, Sylvie!" Tanisha shouts right before I hear the click of the cell phone being snapped shut.

The next thing I know, the doorbell's ringing. I'm groggy from napping and don't bother moving. My ankle's throbbing, and I know my father'll answer the door: He closed the shop early to stay home with me. A few minutes ago, he poked his head in to see how my ankle was doing and asked if I needed anything. I didn't. He sat on the edge of my bed for a minute. He glanced at my ankle and after a brief bit of silence said, "Well, if you need anything I'll be in the living room." Then he left.

I wish I understood my father better. This isn't the first time he's sat on my bed as if he had something to say and then left without saying it. He did it the day my mother died and the day I graduated junior high. He did it the afternoon my SAT scores came and the morning his tuxedo shop won a citywide award for best service.

I figure it's just his way. But that doesn't stop me from wishing he'd actually talk to me instead of sitting there in silence. When I was little, I'd pepper him with questions, but after a time, when he didn't answer with more than one or two words, I stopped trying. On those rare occasions when he came to me, like he did today, I'd always wait to see if he was going to say anything, and when he didn't, I'd simply let him go. After all these years of not speaking, we've come to a place where we live together but have completely separate lives.

"Sylvie," my father calls down the hall as if he knows I'm thinking about him. "You have a visitor."

I peek over at the clock on my nightstand. School's been out for a while. I'm bummed I didn't make it to the café today, especially since I told Tyler I was definitely going to be there. Assuming Cherise still went with her brother, they'd be done by now. I figure my visitor must be Cherise. Who else would it possibly be?

"Send her in," I holler back, propping myself up in the bed.

"I'm not a her." Adam walks into my room. "I'm a him."

I've got to stop assuming it's always Cherise. Suddenly, I have other visitors. I should be more prepared.

I quickly run a hand over my hair. I'm sure I look atrocious from lying in bed all afternoon. All these years, I've never put too much stock in what my hair or makeup look like. But right this second, I care. At the very least, I wish I had a little lip gloss. Or even some Chapstick. Damn.

"Don't worry, Sylvie." Adam walks over to the bed. "You look great to me."

I wish he wouldn't be so nice. Really. He's making it hard for me to remember that I'm not interested in boys or dating.

"I saw Cherise." Adam puts a stack of papers on the nightstand. "She went to all your teachers and got your homework assignments. I offered to play delivery boy." He crosses over to my desk and pulls out the chair. Obviously, he's decided not to sit on the bed. A good decision. I've been napping and have no idea what my breath smells like.

"Where is Cherise?" I ask. As long as he is keeping his distance, I feel free to talk. My breath will stay in my space. "I thought she might come by."

"She'll be by later," Adam tells me. "She said she had a few things to do this afternoon."

I raise one eyebrow. "Like what?" I wonder aloud.

"She said she had to check something. Phase two or part two. Something like that," Adam says with a shrug and I shudder to think what she's up to. "Cherise is cool. After I took you to the nurse," Adam goes on, "I met her in the hall. She introduced herself to me and asked if I wanted to have lunch. While we were eating, she told me all about—"

"Lunch?" I cut in. I might have spoken a little suddenly, but the outside world is spinning at light speed and I'm trapped in my room with my ankle on a pillow. Cherise doesn't eat with anyone but me. And her shadow, Tyler, of course.

"I like Cherise," Adam admits freely. "We hung out a lot today." I'm stunned. "In fact, we ate together with the whole swim team." Suddenly, he punches the air, full of excitement. "Did you hear I tried out today? It went so well, they offered me a spot on the team right there in the locker room!"

"Congrats," I say, but my heart isn't in it. I should be oozing happiness and excitement for him, but I just can't get over the fact that Cherise ate lunch with Adam and the swim team today. The *swim team*, for goodness' sakes.

I have more than a million questions about their lunch conversation, starting with, "I didn't know you swam?" continuing with, "Did Cherise really have lunch at the same table as Gavin Masterson?" and ending with, "Tyler always eats with Cherise and me. Was Tyler there, too?" (Answers: No, Gavin wasn't at lunch today. And no, Tyler didn't want to join them. He sat alone instead.)

My next question is on the tip of my tongue ("Did Cherise mention astrology?"), but the question never has a chance to be verbalized. I'm effectively silenced when Adam grabs his backpack and opens it up. "Let's do our chemistry homework together," he suggests.

Adam gets out his papers and heads toward the bed. I scoot up a little more on my pillows, not quite comfortable with the fact that Adam's in my room. I mean I've never had a boy in my bedroom before, unless you count the one and only time Tyler came down with Cherise. We were about eleven years old and played a marathon game of Monopoly.

It's really awkward to be confined to bed with some guy your classmates are calling Prince Charming hovering over you. I almost expect him to lean over and try to kiss me. That's what happened in "Cinderella." Or was it "Sleeping Beauty"? "Snow White"? Ugh. Adam has me all confused.

In fact, I so expect a "Prince Charming kiss," that I swear my eyelids droop on their own, my lips begin to separate slightly, just like a movie starlet of black-and-white films. I can't control my own physical impulses.

I wait expectantly as, holding his homework in his hand, Adam moves in closer. And closer. . . .

Five

Even with Virgo in the House of Love,
you are not comfortable making the first step
toward romance.
www.astrology4stars.com

Nothing happens.

I fully open my eyes to discover that Adam's face is nowhere near mine. He stopped at the side of the bed, closer to my feet than face.

He wasn't going to kiss me. I imagined the whole thing. Very unlike me. I must have taken too many painkillers. Shaking my head to clear it, I pick up the papers on my nightstand while Adam takes a seat on the bed.

I feel the mattress dip under him and

when he shifts into a comfortable position, his butt is touching my thigh. He doesn't move. Instead, he ensures that I won't move either by carefully rearranging the pillow under my ankle. I can't possibly inch away now and risk messing up the footrest he's created. I try to relax my thigh, but it's no use. It's tensed up and hard as a brick. He probably just thinks I'm buff. Or at least, that my left leg is very buff.

I'm doing an imitation of my father. Staring down at my hands and not talking. Unlike me, who lets the silence burn, Adam lights a fire.

"Does your ankle hurt?" he asks, tracing the edge of the bandage with his finger. Not when you do that, I want to say. It feels great. Amazing, in fact.

"I needed seven stitches." It's a non-answer answer.

"Your dad told me when I came in," he replies. I feel taken aback by the realization he's not only having lunch with Cherise, but talking to my father as well. "I'm glad you went to the hospital," Adam says. "Bernie said it might have been really bad if you ignored it." Bernie? He's calling my father Bernie?

"Thanks for carrying me to the nurse," I say, changing the subject away from my father.

"You're welcome." Adam smiles. He has an amazing smile. "I can't even begin to tell you how many girls are now pretending to twist their ankles as I walk down the hall." He laughs. It's warm and welcoming and makes me laugh, too. He blushes as he tells me about the crazy freshman girl who threw herself at him and begged him to carry her to the nurse.

"Rumors travel fast." I shrug with a smile. "I hear they're calling you Prince Charming."

"I've been called worse." He laughs again.

Suddenly the room brightens. It's no longer awkward and uncomfortable. I've found my speaking voice, and I ask him what other names he's been called. He shares stories of his old school. Make that schools. Because his father is climbing a corporate ladder, his family moves around a lot. Their last stop was a suburb of San Francisco.

He's glad to be in Cincinnati because he has cousins who live here. Adam also tells me about the swim team tryouts, sharing that he was such a huge bookworm growing up that his parents forced him to take a swim class to be "more well-rounded." He liked it and it stuck. He swims as often as he can and being able to join a swim team makes changing schools all the time a little easier since he knows he can make friends in the group.

"Not every school has an academic decathlon team or an astronomy club," he adds with a grin. "But even at high schools without pools, there's usually a swim team in the neighborhood."

It's at this point in the conversation that I tell him to be wary about Gavin. Adam thanks me for the warning and says he'll keep his eyes open.

Adam asks questions about me and my family. I find myself opening up. Not entirely, but more than I ever have to a guy. I tell him the basic facts of my life. The date of my mom's death. The name of my father's shop. About the science scholarship and what I need to do to win it.

"I can help with the scholarship," he tells me. "Since I got one to UCLA, I have some good ideas on how to make the board notice you."

"It's okay," I say. "Decisions are coming up soon and there's nothing left to do but wait. And keep up my grades, of course. Thanks anyways."

"I'll do my part to make sure your chem grades are tops," he tells me. "I learned a few things at my old school about how to make the experiments more efficient. Tell you what, when you're back in class, I'll show you a few new tricks."

I've had my own chem lab space for so long, I've gotten used to doing things my way. It'll be interesting to see what Adam can add. "Great," I say, then take a quick glance at the clock. We're both surprised to learn that nearly an hour's passed. It's time to get started on our homework.

Since I missed the last bit of today's lab, he shows me his tabulations from today's titration experiment.

Wow.

He did such a great job. His penmanship is neat and tight, I can read every little notation. And he took such careful notes, there's nothing missing from his work. It's a pleasure to study with Adam. Really. I can't say that about anyone I've ever met before. Not even Cherise.

Time flies by, and it isn't until I hear footsteps in the hall that I realize the doorbell has rung, again.

There's only one person in the world

who takes giant, clomping steps like that. She always has.

"How's it hanging, Gimpie?" Cherise bops into the room carrying a small lunch bag.

She stops suddenly, seeing that I am not alone, and then says with a cheery lilt in her voice, "Hi, Adam."

Unlike Adam's gentle maneuver, Cherise plops down on the other side of me, sandwiching my legs between her and Adam. My right thigh is touching Cherise's butt, too, but the effect is entirely different. Unpleasant, really. I tell her to skootch over a bit, and she does, but fails to puff my pillow footrest afterward.

"What're you guys doing?" Cherise asks with a wink, as if we were doing something we shouldn't have been.

I immediately squash that notion. "Homework," I tell her.

Cherise looks over at Adam's titration notes. "Wow!" she exclaims. "Such nice handwriting." She turns to Adam. "Sylvie's handwriting stinks. For someone so detail-oriented, you'd think she'd have perfect handwriting, but *noooo*." I can see where this is headed and it's embarrassing. I have no clue how to stop her, though. Cherise continues the story: "When we were in seventh grade, we took a typing class after school together."

Adam looks at me and I smile sheepishly. I'd like nothing more than to pull the covers over my head.

"The assignment was to type a letter, so we did. Instead of a business letter, we wrote a love letter to the teacher." Cherise starts to laugh. "We thought we were so funny, we typed some up to all the teachers in school and sent them anonymously."

Adam laughs and asks, "Did you get caught?"

"Nope!" Cherise exclaims. "But because we couldn't tell the typing teacher that we wrote the letters, we never got a grade for the assignment."

"My first and last zero," I interject.

"Can you believe it, the whole prank was Sylvie's idea!" Cherise shakes her head.

I accept responsibility with a sigh. Those were the carefree days, before Yale and school and priorities got in the way of having fun. Not that I would want to relive my junior high years, but there were some bright spots. Like the love letters.

After listening to Cherise and Adam chat about the rest of the school day, I decide that it's time for Adam to leave. It's that priority thing again. I'm not in junior high any more and my life is on a track that doesn't include Adam. As cute, nice, and sweet as he may be, he's gotta go. Eight weeks till graduation, I remind myself. No boys, no parties, definitely no spring dances. Just me and my schoolbooks. Doesn't that sound like fun?

"Before I forget," Cherise says to me, interrupting my thoughts, "I brought you some lotions and teas." She opens the lunch sack she's been holding and dumps a few unmarked containers onto the bed. "Hypericum, calendula, and bryonia, to help with healing." She picks up a small box and shows me the tea bag inside. "Rose hips and lemongrass, along with some other herbs to help your body fight infection."

Adam's acting like he never plans to leave. He's opened a tube of lotion and is smelling it.

"What is this?" He seems oddly interested in Cherise's concoctions.

"Calendula. It'll help prevent scarring."

"We wouldn't want her to have a big scar," Adam agrees. He puts a little of the cream on his finger and turns to me. "Want me to put it on for you? I'm going to be a doctor, remember?" The way he asks is really sexy.

My brain snaps. "No!" I shout so loudly the walls vibrate. I didn't expect for it to come out quite that way. "I mean, that's really nice of you, but I don't want to unwrap the bandage yet. That and, I'm seriously tired. I'd like to go to the living room and"—gasp, dare I say it?—"drink a cup of Cherise's healing tea." I'm overcompensating for my outburst by whispering now.

Without reply, Adam's closes the tube and sweeps me into his arms for the second time that day. I learned from the morning's episode not to struggle, argue, or wiggle. Instead, I accept the ride by leaning into his chest and putting my arms around his neck. Our hallway's very narrow and curves once. I wouldn't want him to trip and drop me . . . maybe I should hang on tight just in case.

Cherise follows us out of my room. Adam sets me gingerly on the sofa and asks "Bernie" for a pillow to prop up my ankle. My father flashes me a look that I've never seen before—I think it might be akin to a smile—then leads Adam to the hall closet.

The instant Adam is out of earshot, I signal Cherise to come closer. Since Adam doesn't seem to be in a hurry to leave and I don't want to be rude and kick him out, I need to take advantage of the fact that he's in the hallway.

"Did you tell him about my star chart?!" I whisper to Cherise. "Is he hanging around because you told him that we're destined to fall in love?"

"Of course not," Cherise says as if it's the silliest thing she's ever heard. "He's hanging around because you're a Virgo born on the Libra cusp, and today is Wednesday. I have nothing to do with it." She's smiling ear to ear. "But I couldn't have picked a better match for you if I tried! He's perfect. Perfectly right for you. Adam is your diamond guy, for sure."

"What about the fact that he's going to California for college and I'm going to Connecticut," I counter. "How can my perfect guy go clear across the whole country after graduation?" I'm clearly grasping for straws here. First, he isn't my diamond guy. I don't have a diamond guy. Second, he just isn't. That's all.

"Small details." Cherise shrugs. "These things have a way of working themselves out." She hands me a piece of paper with a bunch of numbers on it. The number 4 is circled in red.

"When I got home from school today, I planned to review your astrological chart. I got caught up in numerology and, well," she raises her eyebrows, "all the signs indicate the same thing. Cross-referencing your solar chart with your Soul Urge number, it's clear that Adam is going to ask you to the Spring Fling Prom."

I'm guessing my Soul Urge number is four, which would explain the red Magic Marker. I have to stop myself from laughing. "Is this phase two?" I ask.

"Of course," Cherise responds in all seriousness. "Phase one was that you'd find your guy on Wednesday and phase two is that he asks you to the dance." She seems so certain of herself. "So? Has he asked you out yet?" she asks. "He's been here for a while already."

"No," I protest. "And he's not going to. We're friends. That's all."

"Sure you are," Cherise says with a wink. "Soul Urge numbers never lie. And according to the rotation of the sun, when Neptune's moon is high in the sky, a guy who loves you and whom you love will ask you to dance."

I know exactly where she is headed. Ignoring the whole, "guy who loves you and whom you love part," I tell Cherise, "There is no possible way that Adam's going to ask me to the Spring Fling Prom today." It's time to enlighten her astrology with astronomy. "Cherise," I say, "hate to burst your bubble but Neptune has eight moons, not one. Your 'high in the sky' theory is meaningless."

Cherise gets a thoughtful look and says, "Now that I am thinking about it, maybe you're right . . ." Her voice tapers off.

"Aha!" I cheer. Oops. My voice was a little loud there. I lower it and continue. "I told you that just because Adam coincidentally started school today does not mean that we are going to fall in love or go to prom together! I knew you'd come around!"

"Whoa. Now you're talking nonsense." Cherise giggles. "You're only right in that he probably won't ask you to *prom* today. Now that I am thinking about it, Neptune's moon isn't high yet, so we have to rely on the Soul Number alone to get us through till then." She nods her head as if she's come to a very important discovery. "Not to prom, yet, but he *will* ask you out for a regular date before the day is over."

Did she miss the part about Neptune having eight moons?

Before Cherise drives me totally batty, it's time to make a deal. I pause for a second and listen down the hall to make sure Adam isn't headed back. It sounds like my father's showing him my baby pictures. I should start screaming like a maniac to draw their attention away from the album, but I need the time to bargain with Cherise. I'm going to have to talk fast.

"Look," I say to Cherise, "I'll make you a deal. If Adam asks me out before today is over, I'll agree to go along with your 'predictions' and give the relationship a chance."

This is the easiest pledge I've ever made. I'm good at math, and the statistical probability of Adam asking me for a date is less than nil.

"You won't intentionally repel him?" Cherise asks, staring at me. "You'll admit that the stars are right? You'll open yourself up to the possibility of true love?"

"Sure. I'll even go to the prom, if Adam asks me to." I pin her with my gaze. Now it's my turn. "However," I begin, "Wednesday is over in another"—I check the clock hanging on the wall—"five hours and fifty-five minutes. If Adam hasn't asked me out by midnight tonight, then you must promise to rip up my star chart, admit that there is no diamond guy in my near future, and that your past predictions have been nothing more than luck." I pause, then add, "Oh, and you have to join the astronomy club with me."

"Done," she says and reaches out her hand for me to shake it.

This is the easiest bargain I've ever struck. Adam has barely been at school yet. He hasn't had a chance to check out the other girls in our class, or the underclassmen, for that matter. This is a bet I can't lose.

How can I be so sure?

The guys who have asked me out in the past, and whom I've turned down, have all been a bit geeky, like me. Adam may like astronomy and chemistry, but he's no geek. Guys like Adam, well, they never, ever, ever, date girls like me. We're good for friend-ships, but not romance. I'm a background kind of girl and we background girls don't get asked out by popular guys. Like Tanisha and Jennifer told me, it took him only one day and he's already the most popular guy in school.

A noise in the hall catches my attention. Back on task, I hear my father rustling around in the closet trying to get the pillow off the top shelf. Adam laughs at something my father says and I'm stunned at the sound of the two of them palling around. Like the tuxedos he sells, my father's usually dark and serious.

"Did you say five hours and fifty-five minutes till midnight?" Cherise asks me with a satisfied grin. I look at my watch again. "Five hours and fifty-two minutes," I reply with an equally satisfied look on my face. "The day's almost over."

"Plenty of time," she retorts and just then, Adam and my father emerge from the hallway. Adam's carrying a pillow.

"Well." Cherise gives me a wink. "Since I can see you're being taken care of, I'm gonna dash." She obviously intends to leave Adam and me alone.

Cherise gives my father the tea bag and directions to prepare it. My father's used to Cherise's teas and doesn't bat an eye at her instructions. He just nods and assures her he'll take care of it.

Her plan fails. As Cherise is leaving, Adam says, "Actually, I've gotta run, too.

Wait for me, Cherise. I'll walk out with you." He comes over to the couch and kneels down beside me. He gently sets the pillow from the hall closet under my foot. Adam gets his backpack from my room and heads to the apartment door where Cherise is standing.

She appears oddly unconcerned when she should be worried. It's over. I win.

My father's in the kitchen. There's no way Adam's going to ask me out now. Not with everyone around. Plus, he's clearly leaving. He even says good-bye. I make a big show of announcing that I'm going to take another painkiller then go directly to sleep, just in case he plans to call later. Not that I believe he will, I just want to make certain he won't.

Adam opens the door. He steps one foot out into the hall.

Fire up the paper shredder! My star chart is about to get torn up. I hope Cherise is interested in black holes. She's going to be studying them with me in astronomy club Monday night.

I'm so certain that I've made a date-free getaway that I'm completely thrown off guard when Adam suddenly turns back to me and casually asks, in front of everyone, "Want to go out Saturday night?"

I'm completely stunned. I make him repeat the question. "What did you say?"

"Do you want to go on a date with me Saturday night?" he asks again.

I feel the blood drain from my face. Cherise on the other hand has turned pink, her skin glowing with utter joy at having made a lucky guess once again. Although now, I suppose, I am going to have to call it a prediction, without the quote marks and added sarcasm.

"Sure," I tell Adam, with a tinge of resignation. In another time and place, I really would love to, but now isn't that time or place. Not so close to the end of school with so much in the balance. Then again, a promise is a promise. I told Cherise that if Adam asked me out today, I'd go. And I will. I promised that I'd open myself up to the possibility that this could be the "right" guy for me and . . . sigh . . . I will. If things don't work out, then you can blame someone else because I won't intentionally repel him. I swore I wouldn't and I am good to my word.

The bummer of this all is not the date. For

a split second, I look across my living room, into Adam's gorgeous eyes, and think: This certainly isn't the worst deal I've ever made with Cherise. Not by a long shot. . . .

The bummer is that now I'm going to have to listen to her boast about how her astrological predictions are all true. She's going to tell me that I met Adam because today Mars moved into Gemini. She'll remind me that the number 4 was responsible for my date Saturday. Cherise is going to constantly say that I will be getting a dance invitation when Neptune's moon (any one of the eight) is high in the sky. And how, now that the stars have proven themselves once, I can rest assured, they will again. I suppose I should go ahead and buy myself some dancing shoes.

From her place by the door, Cherise gives me her best I-told-you-so look, then turns to go. She and Adam are leaving together, but before she takes off, Cherise can't resist the opening of the bragfest. She turns back and mouths for my eyes only:

"It was written in the stars."

Six

You have the qualities of a lawyer, critic, or scientist with your critical observations and quick wit. Your partner needs to be as smart, diverse, and interested in the world as you.
www.astrology4stars.com

If anyone had told me how much fun dating could be, I might have started a long time ago. Nah, that's not true, but what is true is that I'm having a blast with Adam and we haven't even gone out on our official Saturday night "date" yet.

Apparently the word "date" means many things. I know because I looked it up in *Webster's Dictionary* last night. (So I'm completely neurotic . . . what's a girl to do?)

According to Mr. Webster, there is the "date" on the calendar. Then there is the kind of "date" that means going somewhere at a specific time. In my case, this kind of date would be the romantic appointment on Saturday night, though Adam hasn't told me specifically what time to meet or where we are going.

Then there is a third kind of "date," the one we casually call "dating." It's a transitive and intransitive verb form meaning, to go out with someone regularly either socially or romantically.

Oh, there is also the fruit. "Date" being a noun meaning a sweet, small oval-shaped fruit with a large, narrow seed.

I'm excitedly anticipating the "date" night out, avoiding the fruit because I'm allergic, and I am actively participating in the verb.

Adam and I are officially dating. I mean, Jennifer and Tanisha said we were, and when it comes to gossip, they are definitely to be believed.

Today's Friday and already, I can hardly recall why I've avoided guys all these years. The fact is, with a guy like Adam, I am quickly discovering that I can have it all:

the boy, the grades, the job, and the scholarship focus.

It's been a whole two days and I haven't slid down the slippery slope of dating—when girls lose their minds over boys. Hours spent at the mall buying makeup and new clothes. Instant Messaging instead of homework. Text messaging in class. Study sessions with no studying. Late nights out at parties. Grades dropping. College scholarships drifting away. That steep tumble that I've been actively and effectively avoiding.

Now I think the slope might not be so slippery after all. I mean, I've text messaged with Adam, but it hasn't been for no good reason or during teacher's lectures. My study sessions with Adam (all two of them) have been full of actual studying. There have been no late-night parties (so far) and well, I did great on the one quiz I had this morning. In the couple of days that I've known him, I've discovered that Adam actually pushes me to work harder. Isn't that amazing?

I feel like I have a firm grip on this dating stuff. To use an astronomy metaphor, I have been rotating as smoothly as Earth around the sun. Perfectly on my orbit and not too close to get burned. But not too far to cool things entirely either. My thanks goes out to Galileo for giving me the ideal analogy.

If things continue like this, which according to Galileo's heliocentric theory, they must, I might even be psyched to go to Spring Fling Prom with Adam. If he asks that is.

While I've been "dating," Cherise has been busy working on a chart of Neptune's moons to let me know when the big ask will happen. She says she'll have it ready this afternoon and will bring it by the tuxedo shop. I told her I'd be busy. She didn't believe me.

"Ahem."

Huh?

"Ahem." It's Cherise clearing her throat. "Sylvie, what are you doing?"

"I'm—" What was I doing? Oh yeah. I'm in the school cafeteria having lunch with Cherise (and Tyler, of course, but as usual, he's not talking. Today, he's busy making a sculpture out of his mashed potatoes.) Cherise has caught me staring out the cafeteria window.

"Nothing," I say, because it's darn obvious that I wasn't actually doing anything. "I was just thinking."

"About Adam and the Spring Fling Prom?"

Cherise really is the best guesser, I mean predictor, on Earth. She could have her own call-in radio show and make a fortune.

"Well . . . ," I admit. I can't help but look across the caf and smile.

When I got to school this morning, Adam was waiting for me on the steps leading into the building. My heart skipped a beat when I saw him standing there wearing khaki pants and a light blue jacket. Now he's taken off the jacket, revealing a tight-fitting graphic T. I am honestly going to have to see a cardiologist if he doesn't put his jacket back on soon. Missing one beat was plenty of excitement—that T-shirt is way too much for one small organ to handle.

Adam was sitting with us, but now he's gone and he's . . . table hopping, for lack of a better phrase. He's over at the swim team table now, but I've tracked his progress through a number of different social groups. The cool thing about Adam (one of a growing list) is that he's attended so many different schools, he knows how to make friends fast. He doesn't feel bound by social groups or cycles of popularity. He's as comfortable with the math students as with the cheer-leaders. I wish more people were like him.

He's simply perfect. Perhaps even too perfect. Can a guy be too perfect?

Today, like yesterday, he's been helping me around the school. Carrying my books while I navigate the hall on my crutches. Bringing me water and snacks. Dropping me off at class, making sure I am comfortable before heading off to his own classes . . . that kind of stuff.

Cherise is beaming with pride at how this is all unfolding.

Just a little while ago, when Adam guided me into the lunchroom, the whole swim team was already eating together and they started calling: "Hey Adam!" and "Come on over here."

"Let's go, Sylvie," Adam said as he started heading over toward his teammates. I started toward them but then I saw Gavin Masterson scoot over on the long bench to make room for us right next to him.

"No thanks," I told Adam, frantically scanning the caf. "Cherise's waiting for me."

"You and I sat with Cherise yesterday." Adam reminded me how he sat with us, for-saking his swim team pals. "Let's sit with the team today." Adam gave me his most persuasive grin. It's hard to turn down that grin. It puts butterflies in my belly. "Maybe you'll make some new friends."

I looked over at the swim team guys. Gavin Masterson waved at me. There was a sparkle in his eye that immediately reminded me why I don't like him. It's as if he's constantly planning to do something evil.

I turned away and, luckily, it was then that I saw Cherise and Tyler sitting at a table by themselves. "Maybe next week," I told Adam. "The table seems pretty crowded and I need extra room to put up my ankle." I hobbled on my crutches over toward Cherise.

Thing is, Cherise probably wouldn't have said anything if I went with Adam to the swim table. I think she'd encourage my relationship with Adam over honoring her feud with Gavin. But I can't do it. There's no way I'm eating lunch with the swim team. Not today or ever.

I don't mind if Adam wants to eat over there, though. I mean, he *is* on the team and all.

Adam carried my lunch for me and set it next to Cherise. Then, he hung around for a little while before heading off to circle the cafeteria, eventually landing at the table with his team, taking residence in that empty seat next to Gavin Masterson. Gavin immediately put his arm around Adam and drew him in close for some kind of private joke.

And yet, being as perfect as he is, before he started his cafeteria tour, Adam whispered a reassurance to me that he's only friendly to Gavin because of the swim team. It's not like he plans to become best buddies with him or anything like that.

Lunch is nearly over when I decide to talk to Cherise about what I've been thinking.

"Cherise," my tone comes out more anxious than I'd like, "for one minute, I don't want you to read the cosmos. As my best friend, I simply want your opinion. You have known me most of my life. This whole Adam-and-me-relationship thing is too weird. I just don't get it."

"Would you believe me if I told you the planets had an unseen vibration that radiated from their geometric positions on the day of your birth at the moment of your first breath?"

"Please, no," I tell her, putting up one hand to stop the mumbo. "Is there any *other* reason Adam might want to date me? Any other reason at all?"

"How about this: You're likeable," Cherise says.

I'm not convinced. I think that maybe she's telling me what I want to hear instead of what she believes.

"I like you," she prattles on. "And Tyler likes you." At that Tyler raises his head. He looks at me sideways as if checking out a car wreck, something you don't want to see, but can't help staring at regardless.

"Come on, Cherise," I beg. "Adam seems to have no faults at all. He's cute and popular and athletic with just the right mix of nerd thrown in. There must be a reason, a real reason he's picked me over all the other girls at school." I pause and glance over at Adam, who's having some kind of milk-chugging contest with Gavin. The guys at the table are going wild. I can hear them shouting Adam's name.

I take a deep breath and remind myself that he has to be friendly to the team captain.

Cherise puts her fork down. It clinks against the table. "Face it, Sylvie, Adam asked you out because the time was right."

"Do you mean that if Mars wasn't in

Gemini, Adam wouldn't like me at all?" This isn't the answer I expected. I feel a little creepy. Like Cherise is saying that Adam is attracted to me against his will.

"Don't be silly," she reprimands. "If you met last week, he'd still like you. He just wouldn't fall in love with you."

Now I am feeling even more creeped out. Does Cherise really believe that Adam is some planetary puppet? I regret having raised the subject. I'm not sure how I expected her to answer my question but this wasn't it.

"If Adam doesn't like me on his own, then this deal is off. I'm going back to guy-avoidance mode and cancelling our date Saturday night."

"Don't worry so much," Cherise tells me. "The stars set things in motion. That's all. You both can ride your destiny, or avoid it. Up to you."

I guess I get it. Kind of. "So," I say, to be certain, "you believe that Adam and I met on Wednesday because of the stars, but he didn't have to ask me out, and I didn't have to say yes. We could have stopped the train at any station?"

"I knew you'd understand!" Cherise is

glowing with pride and happiness. For her, this is the instant that I, Sylvie the Scientist, come to understand astrology.

I don't buy it, but I have committed myself to go along with her stars theory. Being my obsessive self, I will continue to wonder why Adam has chosen me, of all people on Earth, or at least in this school, to go out with this Saturday night.

Looking over at Adam, I see that he's headed my way and once again I wonder if he's just too perfect. If I had put everything I wanted in a guy, looks and personality, into a computer, Adam would have popped out. He's *that* perfect. He doesn't even bite his nails, or smoke, or do anything obviously destructive.

"Ready to go?" Adam arrives and begins to gather up my books. "The bell's about to ring. It's time for the next period." Add punctuality to his list of attributes. And politeness, as Adam nods to Tyler and asks how he's doing.

"Fine," Tyler replies curtly. "Gotta dash." He jumps up and slips on his black jacket, which blends in with his black pants and shoes and shirt. His skull-and-crossbones earring shimmers in the fluorescent lighting.

"Later," Tyler says to Adam, me, and Cherise as he vacates. Four words. That's all Tyler said the entire lunch period. When Adam helped me settle in at the table, Tyler didn't respond to either of us, even though we both greeted him. I've never understood Tyler and frankly, have never really tried. Though on some level, he's always intrigued me. Not enough to try to talk to him, but just enough to make me curious about what more there is behind his black exterior.

Acting once more the prince, Adam guides me to standing, careful to avoid bumping my ankle. His lovely eyes are bright and there is a warm sincerity in the way he's helping me. He even clears my tray. As Cherise reaches for her brother's deserted plate, I'm suddenly curious about what Tyler was creating with his potatoes.

It's a mashed potato star.

And he left his fork stabbed directly into the middle of it.

Seven

Loosen up and enjoy the moment,
there is always room for critical thought later.
www.astrology4stars.com

I'm in the shop, hemming pants as usual, when Cherise arrives. We're alone once again. My father had run to a supplier for more black thread. Being a tuxedo shop, we go through a lot of black thread.

Cherise has come to tell me exactly when Adam will be asking me to the prom. But first she wants to know, "Where are you guys going Saturday night?"

I shrug and for an instant wonder if it's a bad thing that here it is Friday afternoon and Adam and I haven't firmed up our plans for tomorrow night. "We haven't talked about it," I tell her. "Adam said he'd be in touch after swim practice today."

"That's exactly what I hoped you'd say," Cherise cheers, grabbing a chair and pulling my astrological chart out of her book bag. "I have something to show you."

I can't help it. I roll my eyes. I'm trying so hard to be accepting of all this. The eye-roll was a throw back to BD (Before I made the Deal with her regarding Adam asking me out). BD, I permitted myself to make fun of Cherise's hobby. Now, I must reprimand myself and silently promise to try harder to keep my cynicism under control.

Either Cherise doesn't notice my slip, or she doesn't care. "I was reviewing your chart," she says.

"The solar or natal one?" I cut in. Just to show how much I'm trying, I've taken to using her lingo. If I'd won the deal instead of her, I'd fully expect her to be spouting astronomy terms. Fair is fair.

"The natal one," she tells me while unfolding the large familiar white paper with its big hand-drawn pizza circle. The chart is looking well-worn. The paper's now wrinkled and battered around the edges as if she'd been folding it and unfolding it frequently. Studying it. Memorizing it. Preparing to make more predictions about me with it.

Cherise spreads the paper on my sewing table, knocking a spool of thread to the ground as she runs her hand over the page to smooth out the creases.

"See here, Sylvie," she begins. Cherise has graduated from pointing at the chart with a simple pen, to some long fancy wooden pointer thingy with a cast silver hand on the end. The pointer part is a little hand with its first finger out and on the wee mini-nail is a small purple stone. I interrupt to ask Cherise where she got the pointer thingy and she tells me it's a Jewish ritual object for reading the Torah, the first five books of the Bible written in scroll form.

Cherise isn't Jewish and doesn't own a Torah, or a Bible in any form. She's told me before, "The world is my religion, the Earth my goddess." Since my father has never taken me to a church, synagogue, or mosque of any kind, ever, who am I to criticize another person's beliefs? We're Christian, even though we never go to church. The only religious holiday we celebrate is Christmas. Cherise's family commemorates

Christmas, too, although Cherise would never say it's because she's Christian. Cherise chooses to call their tree a "Universal Evergreen of Everlasting Love." Whatever.

"I think the pointer adds dignity to my astrological reading," she informs me. Then adds, "Nathan Feldman lent it to me. He got it for his bar mitzvah. I think he's still trying to get up the nerve to ask me out." I laugh because Nathan Feldman has been trying to ask Cherise out since kindergarten. He often hovers, mutters, and retreats. Sometimes, he gives Cherise gifts or stuff for her to borrow as conversation starters, like today I suppose, when he lent her the pointer. Sometimes I just want to shake him and shout, "Get it over with already! Ask her out!" But I don't and he won't.

I'm of the opinion that by using the pointer on an astrological chart, Cherise is practicing some sort of sacrilege or mocking a Jewish religious object, but she looks so serious, I decide that voicing my concern would be tantamount to throwing our friendship out the window. I know with certainty that Cherise respects all people equally. There's no way she'd intentionally mock someone's faith.

"Nice purple stone," I remark instead of saying what's on my mind.

"Thanks. It's amethyst, the stone of intuition." She grins. "Now, about the prom. You can see that Aquarius is in your Fifth House." She taps one of the drawn pieces of pizza with her pointer. "This is the house of Creativity and Sexual—"

Saved by the bell. The shop's doorbell, that is! I don't think I could have shot out of my chair and grabbed my crutches to answer the summons any faster if there was a supernova explosion under my feet.

Emerging from the back room, I discover Tanisha and Jennifer standing by the wedding dress. Once again, admiring it and probably dreaming about their own eventual nuptials.

"Hey," they say simultaneously as I approach, slowly swinging on my crutches.

I don't even have a chance to utter a few generic niceties before they launch into why they're paying me another unexpected visit.

"Did you get a chance to look at the costume designs?" Jennifer asks.

"Yeah, did ya?" Tanisha leans in toward me.

"I—" Hmm. Not sure what to say. I still don't have time to make those dresses, no matter how pretty they are. Then again, I suppose if I *was* going to the dance with Adam, I would like to wear the Cinderella costume, the whole "Prince Charming" thing being such big deal around school. The costumes would be glamorous and make a comedic statement at the same time. "I . . . ," I begin again.

"What costume designs?" Cherise sticks her head out of the back room where she's clearly been eavesdropping on the conversation.

"I . . ." I'm starting to sound like a broken record.

"Ohhh," Cherise says suddenly. I see her standing taller as she realizes that these "designs" were the reason Jennifer and Tanisha came into the shop this past Monday. And with that dawning realization, comes the knowledge that she saw me stash the drawings behind my father's desk. Where they have remained ever since.

Cherise is behind the desk in a flash. Seconds later, she emerges with Jennifer and Tanisha's three sketches in her hand.

"Wow," Cherise says as she studies the wood nymph and its wings. "Oh my," she gasps after seeing the Old English gown with its velvet and lace. And when she flips the page to the third, Cherise, for possibly the first time in her life, is speechless.

We all stand silently watching, waiting for her to speak. When she finally opens her mouth, Cherise dramatically clutches the pages to her chest, holds them against her heart, saying, "You *have* to make these costumes, Sylvie. You just *have* to."

Jennifer jumps in. "Tanisha and I are road tripping. We've decided that to make these costumes work, we need to visit the best fabric store in all of Ohio. It's a little shop near Case Western called Maude's Materials."

"I went there once with my mom when I was a kid," Tanisha adds.

"My dad's at a conference in Cleveland, so we're catching the bus first thing in the morning and he'll drive us back home early Sunday afternoon," Jennifer tells us. Turning to me, she says, "We were going to buy the material as a surprise for you." Jennifer is so pleased with herself, she's glowing.

Tanisha adds, "While we're in Cleveland, we're going to tour the Case Western Reserve's theater department. We've both been accepted to go to Case next year to study theater arts and costume design."

"After we graduate, we're going to open our own custom costume design shop."

Jennifer puts in. "We'll call it 'J T Designs.' Isn't that the bomb?"

"Yeah," I softly echo. "The bomb." I still haven't agreed to make anything and already I'm feeling an unwelcome amount of pressure. "Look," I tell them. "Your costume designs are really good, but I've no idea how I could possibly make them." I mean I've already added a boyfriend to my very busy schedule. Making three dresses might be just the thing to put me over the edge.

"She'll do it."

My head spins entirely around in a move made famous by *The Exorcist*.

Cherise drapes one arm loosely around my shoulder and pulls me into a private corner. "The dresses are part of your destiny," she tells me. "It's no coincidence that the Fashionistas have handed you these drawings and asked you to create the costumes. It's all part of what I wanted to show you this afternoon."

With one hand on my back, Cherise leads me back into the sewing room, motioning for the other girls to join us. My crutches propel me forward as she escorts me back to my chair and picks up her Jewish pointer thingy. Jennifer and Tanisha have followed, obviously curious as to what Cherise wants to show them.

The whole Tanisha "fox purse incident" is apparently forgiven or perhaps forgotten the moment they get a first glance at the astrological chart Cherise's drawn for me. For some crazy reason, the chart seems to raise her in their esteem. They don't even seem to mind that she keeps referring to them as the "Fashionistas." I think they might even like it.

Cherise quickly brings Jennifer and Tanisha up to speed in the predestined saga of Sylvie and Adam. I can tell by the looks on their faces, they are eating up this romantic tale of literally star-crossed lovers. She tells them that due to my Soul Urge number, 4, he's asked me out, but that we haven't determined where we're going.

"Now, look here," Cherise says, indicating a place on the chart with the pointer. "With Jupiter entering Scorpio, Sylvie's love interest will take her to a familiar location and ask her an important question."

"Cool," gushes Jennifer, as she leans closer in to get a better look at my star chart. She asks to borrow Cherise's pointer and then, as if the document is some rare, ancient piece of parchment, gingerly touches a pencil-mark notation that Cherise has made on one side of the pizza. "What's this?" she asks.

"According to my mathematical calculations," Cherise begins (and I'm wondering what Mr. Weston would say if he knew this is how his top math student is using her knowledge.) "Jupiter is moving into Scorpio at 7:03 Eastern Time tomorrow evening. Therefore, the important question will reveal itself between tomorrow night and noon on Sunday, when Jupiter will push forward into new territory." She also explains how at the same time, coincidentally, one of Neptune's moons will be on the rise. A specific indication that dancing is in my future.

"Well then, it's a done deal," Jennifer says, standing up straight and stepping back from the chart. She hands Cherise her pointer. "Adam's going to ask Sylvie to the prom tonight." They're talking excitedly as if I'm not in the room.

"I get it." Tanisha leans over the chart as if all the secrets of the universe are written there. "The love interest is clearly Adam. And the question will definitely be 'Will you go to prom with me?'" With her hands on her hips, Tanisha stands up and declares, "We can triple-date to prom together! Now there's no reason for you not to make the dresses."

"Oh, please," I retort. "I'd actually like it

if Adam asked me to go, but I'm not going to agree to make three dresses in the next four weeks. As of now, I have no date and no time and I'm definitely not making this commitment based on how Jupiter is cycling."

Cherise taps her chin with the pointer hand. "After Adam asks the important question, you will explore unexplored possibilities. Love *must* be that possibility because you've never explored it before." Her voice becomes stronger, louder. "The chart's meaning is obvious. By the night of the Spring Fling Prom, Sylvie will be in love."

We're back to where we started the day I lost my mother's diamond, when Cherise first predicted I'd be falling in love. I mean, dating Adam has been nice and all, but it's not the same thing as falling in love. This isn't some fairy tale.

"Where are you going Saturday night?" Jennifer asks me. "It has to be a familiar place, right?" She looks to Cherise, who nods in agreement.

"I've no idea yet. And anyway, Adam might choose a new restaurant. Somewhere I've never been before. What would that do to your prediction?" I ask Cherise.

"He won't," is her reply and before I can

counter again, my cell phone messaging alert goes off. I get up from my chair and skipping the crutches, hop across the room to grab my phone out of my purse.

It's Adam.

I'll pick you up at 6 for dinner. Movie after.

I reply with lightning-fast texting skills.

OK

I feel Tanisha, Jennifer, and Cherise gathering around me to read over my shoulder.

"Ask him where," Jennifer tells me, right before I press the send button. I add:

Where?

I hope beyond hope that he says the name of a place I've never heard of. We're all crowded around my phone's little screen not so patiently waiting when the message is returned.

The Krnr Cafe.

And with that the conversation ends. I shut the phone and turn to face three high school seniors wearing identical grins.

"The Corner Café," Cherise says, her smile so wide her cheeks touch her ears. "Not just any familiar place." She smiles even wider if possible. "Your favorite place!"

"I'm sure I told him I like hanging out at the Corner Café," I tell Cherise. "He probably picked it just to make me happy."

"You can believe what you want to believe, but so far, I haven't missed a single prediction." Cherise turns away from me to face Jennifer and Tanisha. "Now, about those costumes," she says. "You will, of course, be choosing organic materials in colors that have not been tested on animals. Sylvie will need hemp thread and chemical-free batting. . . ."

I flop back into my sewing chair and pick up the tuxedo pants I was working on. Apparently, I'm making Jennifer's and Tanisha's costumes after all. The three of them are so busy planning, any protest I might have would fall on deaf ears.

As I rethread my needle and return to hemming, I consider that if the stars aren't dictating my life, then just maybe Cherise is.

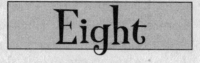

Eight

Identify your emotional boundaries and only then will you be able to move beyond them.
www.astrology4stars.com

It's date night!

I told my father I'd be late getting home. He didn't sound happy about it, but he didn't ask why either. I kind of wish he'd asked me where I was going. He probably forgot Adam asked me out and thinks I have a school thing or am going out with Cherise.

I'd like to tell him about Adam, the star signs, and basically . . . I'd love to tell him everything. Really. I mean, he was young once and used go out on dates, right? He dated my mom for sure. Maybe he remembers some stuff that would be useful to me. When he met Adam the day I cut my ankle, it seemed like the two of them got along pretty well. It would be so cool to sit down with my father and have a conversation about Adam. Or school. Or college. About Mom. Anything, really.

I'd like to walk into the tuxedo shop and say, "Hey Dad, got a minute?" but I won't. I've never done anything like that before, so why would I now? I'm already seventeen. A therapist might say that I don't think he's interested in me (true) or that I'm afraid of rejection (also true). He might even suggest that knowing my father never wanted kids has put our relationship on uneven footing from the start, and he'd be right about that, too. For all these reasons and more, I'm not initiating a conversation with my father.

At least I have Cherise to talk to, even if she is driving me nuts at the moment.

The Corner Café is really close to my apartment. I wanted the independence of going out on this date without my father hovering at the front door, so I e-mailed Adam to tell him that he didn't need to pick me up; I'd meet him at the café at six.

It took the e-mail, a few strong text messages, and one long phone call to convince him I could manage getting there by myself since I'm still on crutches, but in the end, Adam agreed.

I feel great. Happy. A little nervous. I've checked my teeth fifteen times to make sure there isn't food stuck in them. I even opened my mouth really wide to check out the side and back teeth. I know it's weird, but I hate it when food is stuck and no one tells you. Cherise usually checks for me, but since she isn't going to be with me tonight, I have to perform my own tooth check.

Cherise came by and did my makeup. I like the way I look. Especially the way my lips are shining. Cherise used an organic lip gloss that is supposed to make my food-free teeth look whiter. I have it in my purse.

Feeling good, I walk, or crutch-swing, into the coffee shop, all dolled up and ready for Adam and my first official "date" (used in this instance as a noun meaning romantic appointment).

"Sylvie." I hear my name called from a back booth. "Over here."

It's him. I secretly breathe into my hand to check my breath. Not minty fresh (I forgot my gum at home), but not stinky either.

"Hi," I say as I head over to the booth, moving slowly. I'm not taking any chance that I might get my crutches twisted and fall. I'm wearing a new-old skirt (thrift-shop old, new to me) and I don't want to get tangled in it as I crash to the ground. Adam is so perfect, for one night, I'd like to be fault free, too.

Adam gets up from the booth and comes over to me. "Let me take your purse." He places the warm palm of his hand on my hip to steady me while I slip the ornate Chilean tote off my shoulders. (You can guess who gave me the purse. The proceeds went to help rehabilitate prostitutes.)

"Heavy," he says. "What on earth do you have in here?" Should I tell him about the rocks? Just kidding, it's probably heavy from the all those makeup products Cherise sent along in case I need a touch-up. She didn't just send the lip gloss. I have a whole arsenal of paraben-free cosmetics in my bag.

"You should have told me your purse was so heavy," Adam admonishes. "I'd have met you at your apartment and carried it for you."

He clearly hasn't gotten the message

that I didn't want him at the apartment.

"It's okay." I slide into the booth. "Once I found my balance, I didn't have a problem."

"Nonetheless," he insists, "next time I'll help." The way he says it makes me feel good, not like he's pitying me, but like he really wants to be there for me.

I make an immediate resolution just to have fun tonight. Not to think about the stars and whether or not Adam and I are made for each other. I'm going to relax and enjoy myself. Tonight there's no Mars or Gemini or Jupiter. No Soul Urge number 4. No deal with Cherise to let love blossom. Tonight, I'm a girl out with a great guy she met in chem lab.

The waitress comes over for our order. Her name is Monika, and she's new. I don't know her all that well yet, but I like her already. A lot. Especially since she's smart enough not to shout out across the restaurant: "Hey, Sylvie. Is that your new boyfriend?" like every other waitress, cook, and busboy who works here. It's so embarrassing.

Monika, bless her, simply gives me a wink. That's all. And one wink is plenty.

I usually order spaghetti. Over the course of a week, it isn't uncommon for

Cherise and me to eat three or four of our major meals here in addition to whatever hunger-buster we choose when we arrive each afternoon.

At the ripe old age of twelve, our parents let us go buy an ice-cream cone at the café all by ourselves (me, Cherise, and Tyler, of course) and the rest, as they say, is history. I often joke that my earnings from the tuxedo shop go directly into the Corner Café's cash register.

Spaghetti is way too messy on a first date, so I order a salad. Adam gets the spaghetti. I'm a little jealous of his order, but he clearly has a dating confidence that I'm lacking. I ask for a Coke. So does Adam. Monika returns with the drinks right away.

"So," Adam asks, "when are you getting off your crutches?"

"I don't really think I need them anymore. The doctor's office is closed today and tomorrow. I have to wait until Monday after school." I fiddle around with the straw in my drink. My sentences feel short, like they don't flow into a conversation. How come I can talk to him so easily at my house and at school, but now, when it's an actual date I've become tongue-tied?

Well, I guess it doesn't take a trained psychologist to know what my issue is: I am scared to death that he's going to ask me to the prom over dinner. Then I'm going to have to contend with Cherise gloating at me, waving her natal chart in my face for the rest of my life. Or, he's not going to ask me to the Spring Fling Prom and I'm going to have to live with the disappointment especially since now I'm committed to making Jennifer's and Tanisha's costumes.

I'm in a conundrum. A complete mess. I'm damned if he asks me to the prom and damned if he doesn't ask. It's no wonder I can hardly form a sentence.

A big part of me wishes he'd simply get his preordained "important question" in this "familiar place" out of the way, so I can enjoy the rest of our evening.

As if on cue, Adam says, "I have a question for you."

It's nearly impossible to accept that things are really about to unfold the way Cherise said they would. I think I might have to come around and accept astrology after all. I mean, if Adam asks me to prom tonight, that will mean that Cherise has hit every prediction she's made on the head.

Maybe there is something to it, after all.

I try to look as surprised as I can, saying, "Really?"

"Yes." He pauses then begins. "Would you like to go to Gavin Masterson's party with me next Saturday night?" Adam asks, then takes a long sip of his soda.

"I—" I can't seem to formulate words to respond. He didn't ask me to the Spring Fling, did he? Forget what I said a second ago. Astrology is definitely nonsense and Cherise has no idea what she's talking about. Prom! Ha! Adam didn't ask me to prom, noooo, he asked me to go to stupid Gavin Masterson's instead. Adam knows I hate Gavin. Everyone knows Cherise and I hate Gavin. This is not going like Cherise predicted. Not at all.

"Sylvie?" Adam's speaking, but my brain synapses aren't firing. I catch a glimpse at the reflection of myself in the café window. It's not pretty. I'm staring at Adam, jaw dropped open. Good thing my teeth look great because he's seeing all twenty-eight of them.

My tongue settles into form, just enough for me to manage to say, "I'm working next weekend."

"Please, Sylvie," Adam is nearly begging. "Come with me after work. I know you don't like Gavin, but maybe it's time to put aside your differences." I look at Adam, who is watching me with anticipation. "I really want you to go with me." He runs a hand through his hair. "There's a swim meet before the party and I was hoping you'd come cheer me on."

I sigh. Maybe he's right. Maybe it's time to forgive and forget something that happened eight years ago. I shake my head as if the physical movement will dislodge the memories of seeing Gavin shove Cherise to the ground right before he stole her lunch money. I shared my peanut butter sandwich with her that day. And every day for the next month. Gavin was relentless in his torture of Cherise, right up until winter break, when he found himself a new victim. (I think a phone call from Cherise's dad to Mr. Masterson might have encouraged Gavin to move on.)

It's amazing how some things are easy to forgive and forget while others become etched in your brain forever and cannot be dislodged. Honestly, this many years later, should I still hold a grudge? The least I could do is try to move past it, right? I honestly think Cherise will understand if I go to the party. She might even support it because I'm going with "my diamond guy."

"Okay," I agree. "I work at my father's shop on Saturdays, but we close at five o'clock." Like he didn't know that already. I mean it is Saturday right now and we met tonight at six, for exactly that same reason.

"Fantastic." Adam picks up my hand off the table and holds it in his. "The meet's at seven," Adam tells me. "Afterward, we'll head over to Gavin's house."

For the rest of the night nothing went as well as I'd hoped, but it wasn't terrible either. I guess my expectations for the evening were way too high. I was disappointed when Adam asked me to Gavin's instead of the dance (totally Cherise's fault) and I had trouble bouncing back.

After dinner Adam took me to see the classic *King Kong* at the Esquire. It was nice that he remembered that I like old movies, but he fell asleep during the best part. Adam explained that he'd had an extra swim practice earlier that day, and he bought me ice cream to make up for it. After, we would have gone for a walk (or crutch-hobble) in the moonlight, but it was too cold. It was too cold to do much of anything so we decided to end our evening early.

Adam walked me back to my apartment building. Then, in the warmth of the building's empty lobby, between a potted fake plant and the brass-colored mailboxes, he pulled me close and kissed me.

I don't have a lot to compare it to, unless you count Jimmy Sanchez in the third grade.

I felt awkward at first. Not knowing whether to close my eyes or keep them open. (I chose closed.) I tilted my head left at first, only to discover that Adam had gone left, too. (Okay, so my eyes weren't totally closed. I was peeking though half-slits.) I quickly reversed directions and then . . . our lips met.

The kiss was nice. Not an explosion of emotion, no fireworks blasting in the background the way they often do in the movies. No, it wasn't like that at all. It was warm, comforting, and well . . . nice.

The evening wasn't all I imagined it would be, but it was just one night. Already, there's another date with Adam scheduled on my calendar. All things considered, the night might have been off the mark, but the guy . . . he's definitely still my perfect match.

Nine

*Your romantic side is struggling against your
analytic side. Allow yourself to see all
the parts that form a relationship.*
www.astrology4stars.com

I'm back. Sitting in the same booth in the
back of the Corner Café as I sat in last night.
My crutches are leaning against the wall in
the exact same place, too. Only this time,
I'm not with Adam. I'm alone.

It's eleven forty-five Sunday morning.
Cherise was supposed to meet me here at
eleven thirty.

Where is she? I'm starving.

The waitress approaches for the mil-
lionth time to ask if I'm ready to order. At

this time of day, the Corner Café is super busy. I'm getting the impression that if I don't order something soon, I should leave and let someone else have the table. The waitress gives me a look that confirms my suspicions.

"Sylvieeee?" Dotty hums my name. "You have to place an order. I know you don't like to eat alone, but if Cherise, or that cutie-pie boyfriend of yours (wink, wink) isn't here in three minutes, I'm going to have to free the table."

"She's ready to order now," a voice says from beneath a black cloak, near the café's front door. It's Tyler and he's wearing . . . I have no idea what to call it. It's definitely a cloak of some sort. He kind of looks like Darth Vader only without the helmet. Or the Grim Reaper without a scythe.

Whipping off the cloak, Tyler hangs it on a nearby coat hook. I've gotta say, the look isn't any better without it. He's still channeling Zorro, all that's missing is a mask. Black T-shirt. Black jeans. Black belt. Black Converse shoes. Sheesh. Tyler never has to separate colors when he does his laundry. He's a one-load guy. (Unless he wears tightie-whities! I struggle to hold back a slight smirk at the thought of Tyler in stark-white underwear.)

The only visible non-black on his body is that earring I gave him for Christmas. The silver shines out from all that dark, winks at me as Tyler crosses to the booth. I watch him make his way toward me. Tyler's a bit taller than me and has these really long legs. He doesn't need many steps to get to where I am. Actually, he's quite graceful. Tyler would never have dropped a flask and cut his leg. He's cool and calm, and his moves appear deliberate.

Tyler doesn't bother to sit across from me like a normal person. Instead he slides into the booth next to me, pushing me over, and snakes the menu out of my hands. Good thing I'd already looked at it. Not that either of us need it. The Corner Café's menu has never changed.

"Cherise's running late," he tells me. "She said she tried texting, but your phone must be off." I actually forgot it at home by accident. "So she asked me to hurry over and hang with you until she can get here. I figured, why not? I wasn't doing anything else." He shrugs. "We're supposed to order her a cheese sandwich." With mustard, no mayo. Lettuce, no tomato. On rye, not white. Chips, not slaw. And a diet Coke. I know the routine. Then again, so does Dotty.

"Where is Cherise?" I ask as Dotty hustles off to grab Tyler a glass of water, giving him exactly one minute to think about what he wants to eat.

"She had to return something to Nathan Feldman," Tyler replies. "His cousin's getting bar mitzvahed next week and he needed it back."

I nod. Since Nathan never says anything to Cherise, at least nothing of consequence, she'll thrust the pointer at him, he'll probably mutter his thanks for a second, and then she'll be on her way. I check my watch: 11:50. I won't have to spend more than ten minutes with the Prince of Darkness—if I'm lucky.

Sitting here with Tyler today is the opposite experience from being here with Adam. Only the booth is the same. I'm not going to check my teeth. I don't care if I have bad breath. My tongue is not tied in knots. And when Dotty returns, pad and pencil poised at the ready, I order my favorite antidate lunch—the messy, saucy, yummy spaghetti.

Tyler orders a burger and coffee. I didn't know he liked coffee. I almost laugh when he orders it black—of course.

We tell Dotty about Cherise's sandwich, then shoot the breeze while waiting for the food to arrive.

He asks about my classes. I ask about his band. Tyler has been playing keyboard for the same band since junior high. None of the other guys go to our high school; they all met in soccer league. When they discovered that they all hated soccer, they dropped the team to form the band. It's called Silent Knight.

I've actually never seen Silent Knight play. If they played somewhere real, like somewhere other than in Tyler's friend's basement, maybe Cherise and I would go to support them. Then again, maybe not. I'm not sure, but since it's never happened, we've never had to decide whether to go or stay home instead.

I have a theory that Tyler's whole alternative rock band thing started as a jab at his parents, who paid for years and years of classical piano training, hoping he might attend Juilliard. Cherise told me that after graduation, instead of going to college,

Tyler and his band are heading to New York City to try to get a record deal. The Gregory parents' college dreams have all fallen on Cherise.

I hate to break it to them, but even though Cherise has applied to the University of Cincinnati she really doesn't want to go there. She has AmeriCorps dreams. She's even filled out the application. Cherise's just not brave enough to tell her rents. Yet.

"So," Tyler says after a lengthy pause in the conversation. "I have a question for you."

"All right," I say. "Shoot." There's none of the anticipation I felt last night when Adam said the same six-word phrase.

"What do you want?" he asks.

"Want?" I repeat. "Oh. That's simple. To go to Yale and study astronomy," I reply, squinting at him, eyebrows drawn together. Not my most attractive look, but I'm baffled. What the hell is he asking? Everyone knows that astronomy at Yale has been my dream. Even people who don't know me well know about the science scholarship. It's all I've focused on for as long as I can recall.

"Dig deeper," he tells me as Dotty refills his coffee cup. "Really, Sylvie. What is it that you truly want, more than anything else?"

Tyler is staring at me so hard, I find myself turning away uncomfortably from his intensely inquisitive gaze.

Suddenly, I feel defensive. Why should I have to explain my personal decisions to Tyler? I mean, astronomy's what I've always wanted. Haven't I lived my life in pursuit of that goal? Isn't it obvious to everyone? Yale's one of the best schools in the country. To get what I want, that's where I have to be.

"I mean, are you sure that's what you want?" he asks.

"Positive," I tell him. "If you have to ask, then you don't know me at all."

"It's not about if I know you," he says with a curt nod. "This is about if *you* know you."

I was wrong. Tyler's not Darth Vader. He's Yoda. "Thanks, but I've got my life meticulously planned out." It's my nice way of saying "Take your pop psychology and back off." And he does. I've unintentionally, yet effectively, ended our conversation.

After a few minutes of uncomfortable silence, the food arrives. Dotty sets Cherise's sandwich on the table in front of where Cherise should be sitting. I check my watch again. She's half an hour late. What could possibly be taking her so long to return the dumb pointer and get her butt over here? I don't have anything left to say to Tyler.

Or maybe, I do.

"Why do you wear only black?" I ask, taking the focus off my own discomfort.

"Ask Cherise," is his reply. Tyler maintains that calm air about him as he deflects my question and takes a bite of his burger. Juice runs down his chin. He dabs it off with a napkin. For some bizarre reason, the maneuver makes me think of vampires.

"Hey," I complain. "I answered your question. You could give me the same consideration."

"You didn't answer," he responds. "Not really."

"Yes, I did."

"No, you didn't."

"Yes—" I stop. This argument is completely juvenile. That and, now when I think about it, really really think about it, I suppose that I didn't give him a very good answer. What do I want?

Astronomy and Yale, right?

I suppose I've never considered the possibility that there was anywhere I'd rather go or anything I'd rather be doing after high school. Just like I assume he intended, Tyler's pushed me to think about my reasons for pursuing what I've always thought were my dreams. And the truth is, I don't really know why Yale or why astronomy.

I've always said that I'm going to follow in my mother's footsteps. Nothing more, no deeper thoughts about the whole thing. But I suppose that constantly repeating that Yale is my lifelong dream simply doesn't feel like enough of an answer.

Since I can't verbalize a comfortable or complete answer to Tyler, I let the question I asked him drop.

I take a few bites of my food. The conversation with Tyler has pretty much ended. Where, oh, where is Cherise? I have never spent this much time (we are going on twenty minutes now) alone with Tyler.

Tyler seems to be completely at ease, forcing me to wonder why I'm the only one who is fazed by the awkward silence between us. After a couple more bites of burger, he leans across me, and I mean over, across, and practically through me, to stick a nickel in the jukebox on the table by the wall.

I've been here a million times and have

never put a coin in one of those jukeboxes. I didn't know they worked.

His whole body is stretched over me. I inhale and pull back into the booth cushion so that our bodies don't touch. I can't help but notice that he actually smells nice. Kind of woodsy, earthy, and clean. (Don't you dare tell Cherise that I thought that. I'll deny it till the day I die.) I'm surprised at the way he smells. I suppose I expected . . . I actually don't know what I expected.

Tyler puts his nickel in the jukebox and very, very slowly (or so it seems) moves back to his own part of the bench seat.

I can't even remember what I was doing a second before he leaned over me. Oh yeah, it's all coming back to me, Tyler and I were sitting in pregnant silence, eating and waiting for Cherise to get here. I lift my water glass to my lips, but stop midsip.

Wait a second. I love this song!

It's an old Elvis Presley tune called "Stuck on You," and it's got this happy, upbeat, fast tempo. I heard it in a movie a few years ago and I've loved it ever since. I even have the original album. I bought it on eBay the same day I first heard the tune.

"This is a great song." I break our

silence with my compliment of his choice.

"Yeah." He relaxes back, leans fully into the booth cushion, and closes his eyes. Oddly, it's not awkward anymore. The mood has morphed from a horrible we've-run-out-of-things-to-say quiet into a comfortable silence.

While the music plays, I take a few more bites of my spaghetti. Drink some more water. There is no pressure to say anything and I don't really feel like talking. Apparently, neither does Tyler. He's still leaning his head back against the booth, imitating the piano parts with his fingers on the Formica tabletop.

When the song's over, so's the mood. It's awkward again.

"When are you going to answer my question, Sylvie?" Tyler asks as he pops the last bite of burger into his mouth.

"I'll answer yours when you answer mine," is my reply.

"You drive a hard bargain," he says with a throaty chuckle. I think this is the first time I've heard Tyler laugh. Ever.

He reaches into his pocket and pulls out a twenty-dollar bill. "Tell Cherise I stayed as long as I could," Tyler says. He slides the money toward me. "I gotta go. Lunch is on me." Tyler slips out of the booth with the same graceful determination he had when he slid in. He gets his cloak from the hook near the front of the café and drapes it back over his shoulders. Then, right before he leaves, he turns to face me.

He's completely across the restaurant, but I can see his facial features clearly. By reading his lips, I hear him as plainly as though he were still crammed in next to me.

"You should figure out what you want," he tells me. Then adds, "I know exactly what I desire." And then, Tyler is gone.

Ten

Today will pass in an overwhelming blur.
Give yourself time to breathe.
www.astrology4stars.com

"I'm sorry I'm late," Cherise practically skids into the booth. She's out of breath. "I ran the whole way here." Looking around, she asks, "Where's Tyler? Didn't he come to tell you I was late? I'm going to kill him. . . ."

"Cherise," I interrupt, "Tyler just left. I'm surprised you didn't pass him on the street."

"Oh," Cherise says with a giggle. She pokes at the bread on her sandwich. "Thanks for ordering for me, but I'm stuffed. Couldn't eat another bite." Cherise, talking a million miles per second, explains that she was waylaid at the Feldmans' by Nathan's mother shoving an empty plate into her unsuspecting hands. Sunday is family brunch day at the Feldmans'.

"It's no big deal," I respond. "Tyler paid. I'll take the sandwich home." If Cherise isn't going to eat it, my father will.

"You should have seen it, Sylvie." Cherise pushes the plate with the cheese sandwich to the edge of the table. That's our signal for Dotty to wrap it up to go. "There were twenty people crammed into a tiny living room. Grandparents, cousins, aunts, and uncles. All related to Nathan. I swear there was enough food for a small nation. They even had fresh-squeezed orange juice," Cherise tells me with complete awe.

Cherise's family events consist of four people: her parents, her brother, and her. She has an aunt in Florida somewhere, but no one talks about her. I think she might be in rehab.

My family is two people: my father and me. My grandparents are all deceased. Both my parents were only children. In my house, it's a family reunion whenever we're both home.

I briefly wonder what it would be like at the Feldmans' on a Sunday morning. Chaotic, I bet. A bit of a pain, too. Maybe annoying, irritating, and embarrassing, depending on what they talk about. I feel a pang of jealousy and sorrow that I'll never know that kind of chaos and embarrassment. Maybe, if I ever get married, I'll have five kids to build up the Townsend family tree.

But first I need a date to the prom. I start to tell Cherise about how the stars have failed her, when she interrupts. Clearly she isn't ready to focus on me yet. Her head is still at the Feldmans'.

"Did you know Nathan's involved in a Jewish social action group that's working to end the genocide in Darfur?"

"Did Nathan tell you this?" I ask, struggling to recall if I've ever heard Nathan's voice. All I can remember are muttered phrases, not actual words.

"Of course not! Nathan didn't say anything," she says, laughing. "His mom told me about it. Nathan goes to meetings twice a week after school at their temple. They write letters, send informative mailings, work with the press, and contact politicians." She's completely jazzed about Nathan's life. I'm waiting, somewhat impatiently, for a break in her word flow, to tell her about mine.

"The best part is, the group was given permission to send one person to New York for the summer to work at the United Nations and lobby the Human Rights Council." Cherise's hands are fluttering, she's so excited about her story. "Nathan was selected," she says, voice rising. "Unanimously!"

Clearly, Nathan must be able to talk, and eloquently, too, when Cherise isn't around.

I was right about that whole family thing. Imagine Nathan's embarrassment as his mother brags on and on about his success to the one girl Nathan wishes he could speak with but can't seem to. It's heartwarming and humiliating at the same time.

I smile at the thought. I can't wait to someday torture my own children in a similar fashion!

"Nathan's going to make a difference in the world," Cherise says firmly. "I can feel it in my bones." Cherise punctuates her prophecy by pulling the straw out of her Coke and taking a long sip from the side of the glass.

This is my opening. Not only is her mouth busy doing something else, but she has just made a prediction, using bones instead of stars, but a prediction nonetheless.

"Cherise," I say. "Can we back up one prediction?"

"What?" she asks, then grins as she gets it. "Oh yeah. I must have had carb overload on the bagels! I totally forgot to ask how your date went last night! Did he ask you to the dance?"

"The date was fine," I say realistically. "But Adam asked me to a party, not the prom."

"Very interesting." Cherise downs the rest of her Coke, then calls for Marco, the busboy, politely asking him to remove our dirty dishes. Once the table is clear, Cherise reaches in her bag and . . . surprise (not!) . . . pulls out my astrological chart.

Since she returned the pointer to Nathan, Cherise is using her finger to indicate areas on the pizza drawing. "Here's Jupiter," she says, half to me, half to herself. "And my math is obviously accurate."

"Obviously," I echo.

She clicks her tongue as she considers what went awry.

"This indicates your love interest." She nods and points at one section of her chart. "And here's his question. Well." She looks up at me. "I suppose the question could have been about the party and not the dance."

"You said it was an *important* question." I'm cautiously trying to point out that for the first time, she might be wrong.

Cherise isn't biting.

"Well," she says, "he did ask you a question and it was in a familiar place." She waves her arms around the café, indicating not only the restaurant but also the booth. "So I wasn't *that* far off."

"But Cherise, the party's at Gavin Masterson's house," I say with a sigh. "Look, I've upheld my part of the deal. I agreed to go out with Adam last night and I'm game on giving the relationship a chance, just like I promised I would, but do I really have to go to Gavin's with him?" I drop my shoulders. "Let's pretend for a second that I believed in true love. I can't actually believe that my soul mate would take me to Gavin Masterson's."

Cherise thinks about this for a minute. "I think it makes sense that he asked you to Gavin's." She takes a long look at my chart before asking, "When's Adam's birthday?"

Strangely, I know. When he was escorting me to photography class on Thursday, he mentioned that he turned eighteen on Valentine's Day. Cherise is going to *love* that, isn't she?

I quickly mumble February 14th, hoping she doesn't make the holiday connection. But she does, of course.

"Valentine's Day!" she exclaims. "What an amazing coincidence! He's an Aquarius and Aquarius is in your Fifth House."

Cherise asks me for a pen. I wish I didn't have one, but I do. I always do. In times like these, it can be a real nuisance to be as highly organized as I am.

Cherise jots down some notes on a napkin. She descends into silent thought for a few more minutes, then says, "I believe that the reason he asked you to Gavin's party instead of the Spring Fling Prom is on account of synastry."

"Is that a real word?" I ask with a half-snicker. "I had a perfect score on my SAT verbal and I've never heard of synastry."

"Look it up, brainiac." She smiles. "Synastry is the comparison of two people's solar charts."

Oh, please. Why can't Cherise finally admit that astrology's bunk and let us move on? I won't rub it in. I swear. I'd just let the whole thing drop. I'd even continue to go out with Adam because he's a good guy. If he asked me to the prom, great. If not, maybe I'd ask him.

"Hang on," Cherise cuts into her synastry lesson. "Don't you dare even consider asking Adam to the dance yourself."

"What? Do you have ESP now, too? How'd you know what I was thinking?"

"I don't." She squints at me. "I *know* you, Sylvie."

Well that explains it, I suppose. Tyler suggested that *I* don't know me, so I'm glad someone does.

"You can't ask Adam to the dance. It says right here that he has to ask you." Cherise points at my astrological chart. "The stars are unfolding your destiny."

I shake my head. "If the stars say I can't ask Adam myself, then the stars are antifeminist." Cherise, of all people, should get a rise out of the antifeminist line. As an astronomer, I know the stars honestly don't prefer one gender over another. The stars don't have favorites! Even making the statement of possibility aloud sounds insane.

"The stars adore women," Cherise tells me adamantly. "Synastry allows us to see the impact men have on the female energy flow."

Is that English? It sounds like English. The words are familiar, but I don't really understand what Cherise is saying.

"Hmm." Cherise makes a low humming noise as she considers the notes she's written on her napkin. "Hmm," she repeats. Then suddenly, without further discussion, Cherise folds up my chart and tucks it into her purse. She hands me my pen before reaching up to take off her necklace.

A strand of turquoise beads loops low around a second strand of clear crystals. In the center of the clear crystal chain, a large hunk of unpolished turquoise hangs from a silver filigree loop. The necklace is beautiful, and must be new, since I've never seen it before. I'm about to ask if it was designed by desolate pygmies in Guyana, when Cherise takes off the necklace and hands it to me.

"You need this more than I do." She tells me to put it on. I protest, but quickly lose the argument. Admitting defeat, I slip the necklace around my neck, feeling its cool weight fall against my breastbone.

"Turquoise," she explains, "is the stone of clarity. When you wear this necklace, your feelings about Adam will rise to the surface." Cherise goes on, "Remember when I told you that the stars only set things in motion, they don't determine action? I think that the reason Adam didn't ask you to the prom is because he wasn't sure you'd say yes."

"I'll go with him," I tell Cherise. I mean she already committed me to making Jennifer's and Tanisha's costumes. No use in wasting a good Cinderella dress.

Okay, the real reason has less to do with the dresses and more with the truth that I kinda want to go with Adam. I like him. A lot. There! I admitted it. Boy, that turquoise sure works fast! (Ha, ha, ha.)

"So why can't I simply ask him myself?" I inquire, rubbing the turquoise beads between my fingers. The stones have warmed substantially in the few minutes I've been wearing them. "If I make the first move, Adam would know, with no uncertainty, I want to go."

"Don't! By the mere act of asking, you

will throw off the balance of the whole universe." There's a wild glint in Cherise's eye. A warning. She seems nervous that I might really go out there and sabotage the *whole* universe on purpose, just for a prom date. I snort as I consider the awesome power and responsibility that I have in maintaining the flow of nature.

"All right," I reluctantly agree. "I'll wait for him to ask me to the prom." Then, as a jab at her initial mistake, I question, "Do you have a new idea of exactly when that might happen?"

"I'll check the Mercury table when I get home and get back to you," she says confidently, not even acknowledging my sarcasm.

It's time to go. We use Tyler's money to pay the bill and after stuffing my father's takeout into my purse, I maneuver my crutches out of the café. I'm headed over to the tuxedo shop.

Jennifer and Tanisha should be back in town by now and are supposed to meet me at the shop at two. In an afternoon replete with strangeness, I'll admit one more oddity: I'm actually excited to see the fabrics Jennifer and Tanisha chose. I can't wait to start sewing.

Eleven

*Fine-tune the balance between predictability
and the great unknown. You'll be glad you did.*
www.astrology4stars.com

I like schedules. Cherise says I enjoy order
to my day because I am a disciplined Virgo.
I say I like schedules because they help me
stay focused on the important things in life.

Now that I'm officially in a relationship,
I can easily see how hanging out with Adam
might cut into my school and homework
time. According to Jennifer and Tanisha, I
moved from "dating" to "relationship" on
Saturday night. When they came over to sew
Sunday, I filled them in. They assured me
that the party invite was a positive step for-

ward, not a setback. It was then that Jennifer declared my new "relationship" status.

A relationship, huh? Well, that changes things. Don't get me wrong, I want to hang out with Adam. I really like him. I just have to figure out how to fit him into my already busy life. I still can't afford to lose even one fraction of a point off my GPA. And so, in order for this relationship with Adam to work without getting in the way of my scholarship dreams, I have created the following agenda:

6:00 a.m.: My alarm goes off. Press snooze.

6:15 a.m.: Get up. Shower. Get dressed.

6:30 a.m.: Eat breakfast with my father.

6:50 a.m.: Brush teeth. Put on shoes. Gather books.

7:00 a.m.: Leave for school.

7:30 a.m.: School.

1:50 p.m.: Ten-minute progress meeting with Jennifer and Tanisha re: costumes.

2:00 p.m.: Meet Cherise (and Tyler, of course) at the Corner Café for a snack.

3:15 p.m.: Work at tuxedo shop.

5:45 p.m.: Dinner with my father.

6:45 p.m.: Do homework with Adam. Really.

9:00 p.m.: Sew costumes for prom.

12:01 a.m.: Sleep.

I typed up the schedule on my computer and made multiple copies. One to tape on my mirror, one to keep in my purse.

I made a third copy and gave it to Adam. Being the understanding guy he is, Adam totally agreed to help me stick to the program as best as he could. He's going to walk with me in the hallway between classes, eat with Cherise and me (and Tyler, of course) at lunch, and then meet me back at the apartment to study after his swim practice ends. This way, we get loads of time together and I can effectively manage my days as well.

Supportive. Yet another one of Adam's finer points. He didn't even laugh at my organizational neuroses or sarcastically call me "Virgo freak," like Cherise did. Then again, after she stopped laughing, Cherise did help me go to the storage closet in the basement of our apartment house to get my mom's old sewing machine.

To make this schedule work, I needed to set up the machine in my bedroom so I could stay up late doing costumes. Since I am still on crutches, Cherise carried the machine for me.

Having made all the necessary arrangements, my alarm goes off at precisely six a.m. Monday morning. As I reach over to hit the snooze button, I fall back asleep knowing that I am on the proper path to personal and academic success. That's my last thought before my father wakes me up at seven fifteen to let me know I'm going to be late for school if I don't get going.

My very first day with a new schedule and already, I'm flying out the door with no shower, no breakfast, and mismatched socks.

Then there's the doctor. When I made the schedule, I'd totally spaced that I had an appointment to get my stitches out Monday afternoon. I'm sitting at the Corner Café with Cherise and Tyler when I realize my mistake. Cherise drives me over in her mom's car, but can't stay. I have to wait at the doctor's, so I'm even later than I would have been to work at the tux shop, which throws off studying with Adam.

The bright spot in this fiasco is that Adam's swim practice ends early so he agrees to pick me up at the doctor and take me to the shop. My growing list of great things about Adam includes the fact that he has his own car. Wahoo.

Walking is my life, unless I have somewhere far to go, then my father believes in the "many merits" of the public bus system. Cherise usually likes riding the bus with me for environmental reasons, but is willing to beg her mom for keys to their hybrid sedan whenever we are desperate.

When Adam drops me off at work, (crutch free!), he reminds me of another thing I'd forgotten when I made my schedule: Tonight's our monthly astronomy club meeting.

A day that should have been well ordered, has fallen completely off track. To fit all the pieces in, I do my homework at the shop while I hem, then eat a peanut butter sandwich in my room while I cut trim for Jennifer's and Tanisha's costumes. By nine, I've got it all done and am ready to go to the astronomy club meeting.

"Can I help carry your telescope?" Adam asks when he shows up at my door, admirably prompt as ever. Adam oozes a calm that makes me feel better after the chaotic day I've had. He's already carrying his telescope bag on his shoulder so I tell him I can manage my own.

"I'll take your tripod, then," he says, picking up my prized three-legged telescope stand and tucking it under his arm. Then, in a spontaneous move, Adam leans in and kisses me lightly on the lips.

This kiss is definitely better than the last one. We're making progress. And you know what will be even *better*? When we kiss under the stars after astronomy club. Perfect guy, perfect night, that's where we'll have the perfect kiss. I know it. The toes-tingling, ultimate kiss must be coming soon. It has to be, right?

Even though I said I could manage, Adam continues to insist he'll carry my telescope, too. I finally give up and let him.

I'm the proud owner of a Hartforde EGH-80DD Observatory Telescope. I bought the telescope and tripod over the summer with my tuxedo shop earnings. I saved for two whole years to purchase this baby. And I mean *saved*. My thrift-store fashion began when I first saw the telescope in the window of a nearby camera shop. I knew I'd need to cut my spending some-where and since there was no way I was giv-ing up the Corner Café, department store clothes went first. Theater movies disap-peared second, and my love for old flicks kicked into high gear since those are always available on cable. Jewelry, cosmetics, and other frivolous items were all sacrificed in the name of the Hartforde EGH-80DD.

Adam's telescope is also a Hartforde model, newer and even fancier than mine, but that doesn't bother me. Adam got it for his birthday from his grandparents. I'm satisfied that I earned my telescope with my own sweat and blood—literally, since I occasionally stab myself when hemming pants.

This Hartforde telescope is an amazing piece of astronomical technology. The 80mm objective lens is so powerful that the high-resolution images appear bright and flawless. An Autofar Computer Controller system guides my eye, helping me to quickly discover about three thousand preprogrammed celestial objects, automatically separating the stars from the satellites. A specialized motor compensates for the Earth's rotation, making tracking objects easy.

I could go on and on about the flip-mirror, eyepieces, the built-in lens, the tripod with bubble level indicator, and the reminder alarm for astrophotography applications, but I wouldn't want to become a bore.

"Hey, Sylvie," Melanie greets me as Adam and I enter the park. Melanie is the daughter of Mrs. Kelsow, our astronomy teacher. She's a sophomore at our high school. I introduce her to Adam.

They have a quick conversation filling each other in on the basics of their lives, then we all get down to the serious business of stargazing. There are fifteen students in the astronomy club and we all gather around while Mrs. Kelsow gives a short lesson about black holes.

Then we break up to see what we can see. Mrs. Kelsow comes by periodically to help if we need it. Adam and I are basically on our own.

First, we look for black holes, then I show Adam the Great Red Spot on Jupiter. Deftly using a chart to guide him, Adam finds an asteroid. I locate a star cluster knows as the Pleiades. Ironically, Adam points out one of Neptune's eight moons and mentions how high it appears in the sky. "It will be even higher on Saturday," he tells me, causing me to nearly choke on my own tongue.

Could it be that Saturday night is the night he'll ask me to the dance? Now I'm thinking like Cherise. I've got to stop that! When he asks, he asks. (*If* he asks, that is.)

Neptune's moon will have nothing to do with it. Of course, now, you can't stop me from wondering about Saturday. . . .

When club time's almost over, Adam takes one last look through his telescope while I'm scoping out the park for the best location to make out. There's an open area over to the left away from the other astronomy club members. No trees will block our view of the evening sky. As we walk by on our way home, the mood will be just right and that's where it'll happen.

"I had a good time tonight," Adam tells me. We are getting closer to my goal and I'm getting a bit nervous. I'm not the type to make the first move. I wish I was, but I can't. I'm new to all this and simply don't have enough courage. So, I'm hoping that if I plan things right, Adam will seize the moment and sweep me into his arms like his namesake, Prince Charming.

I take a couple more steps, then stop.

"Adam," I say breathlessly, turning to face him and stepping in closer.

"Yeah?" he asks. Clearly, he isn't clued in to my seduction.

I'm trying to look as sexy as I can: half-drooped eyelids, pouty lips, cheeks sucked in. I thrust my chest forward because, well, guys like girls with fuller breasts, right? Nature has deprived me, so to make a show of my A cups, I'm standing in a near back-bend. I'm lucky I haven't tipped over backward.

"What's up?" Adam asks. He's not getting the vibe. I'm going to have to say something.

"I—I thought . . . ," I stutter. "I wanted . . ." Oh, damn. I'm just going to have to act. I stand back up, bringing my chest back to normal, and take another step forward.

I lean in, then retreat.

I'm a chicken.

Thankfully, Adam's finally clued in. His lips part slightly as he closes the distance between us. The telescope bags he's carrying slip to the ground. In an amazing gymnastic feat, Adam both sets down my tripod and secures the lip-lock.

He slips his arms around me. I slide my hands around him only to have him suddenly break away.

"I nearly forgot to give you something," Adam tells me, stepping back and bending low over his own telescope bag.

"A present?" I ask. It seems rather early in our relationship for gifts, but if Adam wants to give me a present, who am I to turn it down?!

He hands me . . . a magazine. I take a step back, more fully into the moonlight. No, it's a college catalog. And a scholarship application form.

I gaze at Adam inquisitively.

"UCLA," he says, taking the catalog from me and opening to a page with the corner turned down. "I want you to take a look at their premed program."

"Why?" I ask, flipping it open. There's a small photo of a woman at a chem lab table, holding a test tube.

"I just thought," he points out another photo on that page of kids walking on the Los Angeles beach, "astronomy's a nice hobby. But it's not a career. You're so smart." He smiles warmly. "Maybe even smarter than me." Adam winks. "Have you ever considered becoming a doctor?"

"No," I honestly reply. "I like astronomy. It's always been astronomy."

"Astronomy's okay," he says, "but you could change the world."

"Galileo, Copernicus, flash forward to

Carl Sagan, even Mrs. Kelsow, they changed the world," I counter defensively, feeling as if we might be at the cusp of our first fight.

When I was at lunch with Tyler, he asked me what *I* want. I'm oddly grateful to Tyler for pushing me. I've been thinking about it ever since he raised the question. I want to be an astronomer. More than ever.

"Why astronomy?" Adam asks and thanks to Tyler, I have a good answer ready.

"Astronomy is about not feeling alone in the universe. Studying the stars combines math with beauty and poetry. It's an exact and predictable science all about comprehending the incomprehensible," I passionately tell Adam. I'll tell Tyler the same thing next time I see him. I have a feeling he'll be proud to know I figured it out for myself. (Now, I just have answer why it has to be at Yale and nowhere else. Is it enough to go there because my mom did? I'm not sure . . . but I'm going to figure that out, too.)

I assume Adam will also admire that I'm able to verbalize such a clearly defined reason, but when I'm done, he replies, "You'd have fun in California. We might even see each other around school!" And at that, he gathers me back into his arms and kisses me hard on the mouth.

See each other around school? Doesn't he mean be together at school? Like boyfriend and girlfriend together?

Hmm.

This is not exactly how I imagined things going tonight, but honestly, I don't feel like thinking about the future anymore. I planned this kiss beneath the stars and I'm going to enjoy it.

Eagerly, I tip my face up to his and allow him to kiss me more fully. His mouth is soft and warm and I melt into the sensation. As I change direction, trying to find that magic kissing spark, my mind races and I tell myself that Adam didn't mean to offend me. He thinks I'm smart and simply wants to help me reach my full potential. If I went to UCLA we'd be together for sure. It makes sense, since we're together now.

When we get back to my apartment, I thank him for the UCLA catalog and tell him I'll look at it. And I will. I mean, since he went out of his way to get the catalog for me, I might as well take a quick glance through it.

Adam kisses me one more time before

he leaves. It's tender and slightly more than pleasant. I hold him tight and when the time comes, I feel reluctant to say, good-night.

Like the star cluster Pleiades, our relationship isn't shooting or soaring, but is a constant, continuing to shine brightly.

I'd have kept to my new official schedule on Tuesday, if Adam's swim practice hadn't run over. Apparently, the coach had a cow about losing Saturday's meet and made the whole team stay late to review an Olympic technique known as "the breath every two" for an extra hour. By the time Adam finishes, he's too tired to do homework. He says he doesn't want to give up the whole evening with me (which, of course, made my heart skip a beat) so, during the almost three hours normally programmed for homework, he comes over to watch television. I have to hustle to finish my assignments before he arrives, but I'm certain it's going to be worth it.

We channel-surf for a while, when Adam suddenly cheers, "My favorite movie!" He sets down the remote and settles back into the sofa.

The movie is a horror flick that came out last year. I didn't see it, well, because I'd never pick a horror movie. Ever. I saw one once when I was younger and still sleep with a night-light because of it (that's a secret, okay?). Adam's been so great about doing things I like to do, even spending most of his lunch period with me and not the swim team, I suppose that watching this film is the least I can do.

It's not so bad. Adam holds me during the scary parts and when the film ends, we make out on the couch, until my father interrupts by stomping down the hall. I was grateful that he warned us of his presence since Adam's hand was creeping up my shirt. We jumped back into our own seats and when my father started puttering about in the kitchen, taking his own sweet time to make a snack, Adam decides to take off.

Oh, well. It was past time for me to get to sewing anyway.

After Adam leaves, I'm wound up and a tiny bit scared. Another twenty minutes is spent checking in my closet and under the bed for spooky things and when I finally start to sew, my heart isn't in it. I end up falling asleep over Jennifer's nymph wing, my head on a folding table I'd set up for cutting material. I wake up at three a.m. with a lacy imprint embedded in my right cheek. All in all, even though the schedule failed, it was another good evening. I even think the kissing is getting better. And I definitely would have let him go up my shirt if my father hadn't come into the room.

Wednesday's right on schedule until nine p.m., when my sewing machine dies. I'd barely started working when the thing conked out. Now I'm at a place where there's nothing more I can do on the costumes, unless I want to sew by hand, (which I don't) so I surf the Web and talk to Cherise by Instant Messenger instead. Then, at exactly 12:01 a.m., I go to bed.

Thursday morning I wake up, more determined than ever to stick to my schedule. What's the use of making a schedule if you can't stick to it? Even for one day! I'm going to get back on track and maintain my scholarship focus by adhering to the timetable I've so meticulously prepared. Those counselors at Yale will be extra impressed when they see my stellar grades, especially if they hear that that I kept those grades up and had a boyfriend at the same time. The science scholarship will soon be mine!

Thursday's the day I'm going to prove to myself that the schedule works . . . and it does. I'm on track, right up until the moment that Cherise coerces me into getting my palm read by some wacky psychic.

Twelve

You are stuck in the mud.
Grab a shovel and start to dig.
www.astrology4stars.com

"Forget about your schedule." That's the first thing the psychic says to me when we enter her billowing tent. All right, so it isn't really a tent. It's a converted storefront with a whole lot of fabric draped around. From the outside it looks like any other store on Twelfth Avenue. Just like any other store, except for the neon placard reading: MADAME JAKARTA, PSYCHIC and the flashing image of a hand.

On the inside, however, the shop looks nothing like any other store on the street, or anywhere else in America, as far as I know. The place is decorated like an Arabian tent from the classic film, *Lawrence of Arabia*. There's so much fabric hanging from the ceiling and tacked up against the walls that Jennifer and Tanisha could have saved themselves the trip to Cleveland to buy material for our costumes if Madame Jakarta would have parted with even an eighth of what she has flung around her shop.

To make a short story long, I'd dropped off my mom's sewing machine at the Sewing Emporium on the way to school. When I called Wednesday night in a tizzy, just as they were closing, Wanda Feines, store owner and repairwoman, offered to open early to take a look at it for me.

The tuxedo shop does a lot of business with Wanda. We only do rentals, but Wanda makes custom tuxes on the side. Most of her clients are referrals from us. When my mom was alive, Wanda was her closest friend.

Over the phone, Wanda diagnosed the problem. "The 212v belt is busted," she informed me. She made that assessment without astrology or palm reading. Wanda simply listened to my reenactment of the noise the machine made right before it shut off.

Wanda had to get the part from her second store out in the suburbs. She said I could come pick the machine up after six. They were closing at eight so I had a two-hour window.

Checking my typed schedule, I figured if I dropped off the machine before school, Adam and I could take a brief study break after school, get the machine, and be back before the nightly nine p.m. sew-a-thon. Wanda's sewing machine repairs would fit smoothly into my schedule. I'd barely notice the blip.

So, after I finished reviewing my English notes for Friday's quiz and Adam completed his European History reading, we headed out. Once again, Adam was absolutely willing to support my fixation with staying on task: fifteen minutes to go get the sewing machine, ten minutes to return home. That left us with another hour and thirty-five minutes to go over our chem lab results.

Adam really is the ideal boyfriend. His acceptance of me at my nuttiest makes me like him even more than I already do. I'm hoping like mad that sometime soon, he'll finally ask me to the dance.

It was precisely seven o'clock when Adam and I were on our way to the sewing store.

Which, happens to be next door to Madame Jakarta's Psychic Shop.

Madame Jakarta has been reading palms on Twelfth Avenue for as long as I can remember. When I was young, she was old. Now she's even older. She usually wears some sort of floral-patterned muumuu with a matching turban, but once I saw her in jeans and a T-shirt at the supermarket. That was just plain freaky.

We were holding hands and casually walking to the sewing shop when who did we see coming at us from the other direction?

Cherise. She was with Nathan Feldman and like us, they were holding hands, too!

To say I was shocked would be an understatement.

I opened my mouth to speak, but there were no words. I didn't know where to begin. Luckily, Adam took over.

"Hey, Cherise." He gave her a little hug. "Nathan." He pushed out his knuckles and Nathan butted his own fist against them.

As if seeing Cherise and Nathan together

wasn't enough of a stunner, the fact that, of the two of them, it was Nathan who spoke first, confounded me further.

"Hey, Adam. How's it going?" Nathan said.

Nathan's actually a pretty good-looking guy. Wavy brownish-red hair. Freckles. Glasses. Straight teeth. And to my utmost surprise, he also has a nice voice. Deep. Soothing. Mellow.

"Hi, Sylvie." Nathan opened his arms and gave me a half hug. The kind you give when you aren't sure whether to hug or not.

I know it's rude, but I couldn't help myself. "Excuse me," I said when at last I found my speaking voice. "I need a minute with Cherise."

Thing is, I hadn't actually programmed an extra minute into my plan. To Wanda's and back. That was the deal. No additional time to find out what in the world was going on between Cherise and Nathan. (And definitely no contingency plan for what to do when that one minute with Cherise morphs into half an hour with Madame Jakarta.) Once again, my schedule was out the window.

Cherise and I moved into the doorway of

Madame Jakarta's. I was practically dragging her by the arm. I'm certain she'd have come willingly, but I was asserting my "best friend's right-to-know" clause by pulling her along.

"How?!" That one word got the ball rolling.

"Well . . ." Cherise had a sheepish smile on her face. She glanced over her shoulder to where Adam and Nathan were sitting on a bus stop bench. They were in a heated discussion about something. Maybe sports. Maybe Darfur. Nathan was waving his arms as he talked. And talked. And talked some more.

Once Nathan gets started, apparently he can't be stopped.

"You and Nathan?" I prodded her attention away from Nathan and back to me.

She shrugged. "I was interested in that Jewish group working against the genocide in Darfur. So I called Mrs. Feldman to see if I could go to a meeting, even though I'm not Jewish. She said she thought it was fine and gave me the address of the temple."

Cherise stole another glance at Nathan. There was a certain look in her eye; I think it was pride.

"Turned out, their next meeting was that same Sunday night. So I went and laid low in the back of the room. Nathan was leading a discussion of how to start an Internet petition to send to members of Congress." She rotated on her heel to face me more fully. "A woman named Rachel introduced herself to me and within minutes, she'd dragged me to the front of the room, volunteering the two of us to put up 'Stop the Genocide' posters in local coffee shops. I went with her on Monday afternoon." Which explained why she couldn't stay at the doctor's to drive me home after I had my stitches out.

"Are you getting to the Nathan part?" I asked impatiently. "I'm your best friend. I can't believe you didn't tell me about him!" I felt a bit angry that she hadn't been open with me. Cherise should have told me why she couldn't have driven me home from the doctor. She could have mentioned something at lunch or at the café after school or on the phone or by stopping by the apartment. . . .

When I thought about it, I vaguely recalled seeing her standing with Nathan in the hallway at school a few times this past week. But since that was hardly unusual, I didn't connect the dots. I just assumed he was muttering and lending her stuff her like normal.

"I didn't want to take the focus off of you and Adam," Cherise explained. "I figured I'd have plenty of time to catch you up after Adam asks you to prom. This is your special time, Sylvie. The stars are aligned for you to be falling in love, not me."

I know Cherise was speaking from her heart. It was so like her to think of another's happiness before her own. How could I be mad about that? My anger slipped away on the cool night breeze.

I asked her if she checked her own star signs regarding Nathan. She told me she did, but nothing indicated she'd meet someone special. In her case, unlike mine, it was pure coincidence.

"Go on," I pressed. "I want to hear the rest."

"At the meeting, I went up to Nathan to tell him I was going to help out with the posters." Cherise brushed a loose hair back over her ear. "At first he clammed up like usual, but pretty soon he began to loosen up. After the meeting, he asked me if I wanted to grab a bite. We went to the Corner Café for chocolate cake."

Cherise's face suddenly broke into a full-fledged grin. "He walked me home and we kissed goodnight," she told me. "It was magic." Cherise paused as if recalling the kiss. "Pure magic." With a toss of her head, she floated back to Earth. "Nathan asked me right then and there to go with him to the Spring Fling Prom."

Being totally selfish, my first thought was, How come Cherise gets magical kisses and a date to the prom without astrology? I get okay kisses and no date, though the stars are supposedly "in my favor." It seems grossly unfair.

"I'm happy for you," I told her, burying my selfishness to discover a warmth growing in my stomach. It's that joyful energy surge you feel when a friend shares really great news. Cherise hasn't been on the same no-boy scholarship diet as me, and yet she hasn't had a date in the same number of years. And everyone knows Nathan absolutely worships the ground she walks on, and has for practically forever.

"If you're going to the dance, you'll need a costume," I said. Not that I wanted to squeeze in sewing another costume, but I couldn't make them for Jennifer and Tanisha and not for my best friend.

"Taken care of," she told me. "We're going as doctors from Doctors Without Borders. Nathan's dad is giving us scrubs. We only need a couple of stethoscopes."

"Now that you're going to the Spring Fling," I declared, "I'm definitely going to ask Adam. As a future astronomer, I promise the universe will be perfectly fine. We can double date!" Jennifer and Tanisha thought that I was triple dating with them, but if Cherise was going, I'd rather go with her and Nathan.

The happy look on Cherise's face turned to sudden fear. "You can't ask Adam!" she exclaimed with a shiver. Then softer, "It would be mocking the stars."

"I'm not mocking them, I'm giving them a swift kick in the—"

"No!" Cherise was practically begging. "Look," she said, raising her eyes to Madame Jakarta's neon sign. "I haven't had time to check the Mercury table to find out exactly when Adam will be asking you to the dance. Let's go in and ask Madame Jakarta." Cherise pulled on the shop door.

"She might read palms instead of stars, but Madame Jakarta's definitely in tune with what's going on in the cosmos. I'll pay."

As Cherise stepped inside, I told her I didn't have enough time or energy for more woo-woo.

"It'll be painless," she promised. "And it'll only take a minute. We'll pop in and ask the one question: When is Adam going to ask Sylvie to prom?" She shouted over to the boys to meet us in fifteen minutes at a nearby tea house. "Come on, Sylvie. It can't hurt to ask."

"It can't hurt. . . ." Those are some famous last words.

Thirteen

Look out for love. If you don't see it coming,
it might pass you by.
www.astrology4stars.com

"Forget about your schedule," Madame
Jakarta tells me.

Weird, huh?

Believe me, when she says it, my immediate response is, "That's creepy." How does
Madame Jakarta know I enjoy a clearly
defined schedule? Then again, she might
have seen me looking at my watch and cal-
culating how far off timetable I'll be in my
sewing regimen with this little side trip to
the freak show. I still need to pick up my
machine from Wanda next door.

Those aren't actually the first words that Madame Jakarta said. Immediately upon entering the place she remarked, "Ahh. Nice to see you again, Cherise."

I had no clue Cherise had even been here before. But like the thing with Nathan, I can't be mad that she hasn't told me. I've never been interested in her metaphysical pursuits. Similar to astrology, palmistry would be on the same list of things we usually don't discuss. If she'd brought it up, I'd have made fun.

Cherise introduces me and gives Madame Jakarta ten dollars. Waving her hands wildly, Madame Jakarta flutters around the room, offering tea and candy-coated fennel seeds, and when we decline, she instructs us to each sit down on a huge square pillow. Good thing my ankle is healed. If we'd have come here last week when I was on crutches, I'd have dropped down and never been able to get up again.

The pillows are covered in soft purple velvet, but the inside feels bumpy, like they're full of those little beanbag foam balls. I try to relax, but it isn't happening. Cherise, on the other hand, looks completely in her element. She leans back on her elbows, comfy on her beanbag square.

Madame Jakarta lights a red candle and places it on the table. I recognize the candle immediately. It's the same type of "candle of love" that Cherise put in my bag at her first astrology reading in the back of my father's store. Cherise and Madame Jakarta must shop at the same psychic gift store. Personally, I've no idea where you can buy "love candles" in Cincinnati. It's a pretty conservative city.

The scent of the candle wafts through the air, casting a pungent sweet smell over the already eerie atmosphere. The flickering flame reflects on Madame Jakarta's bulbous nose, highlighting the dark circles under her eyes. Her turban dances as she chants in a foreign (probably made-up) language.

When she finishes her prayer/song, Madame Jakarta drops down in front of me, reaches out, and without warning, grabs both my hands. She pulls me toward her by my wrists. I nearly fall off my pillow. Only my feet remain on the soft velvet. My knees are pressed into the hard, linoleum floor.

Tracing her thumb over the pulse point on my left wrist, Madame Jakarta says in a smoky voice, full of confidence, "I feel the presence of a boy and hear the music of a dance."

Cherise hasn't even posed our question yet, making another oddly psychic thing that Madame Jakarta had said since we entered her shop. Of course, being a student of science, I'm wondering how she knows about the schedule, the boy, and the dance. There must be a logical explanation. I bet the last time Cherise came in here wasn't very long ago. She probably told Madame Jakarta about my situation. Yeah, I reason, that must be it.

Cherise quickly explains what's going on. "I read her star signs and have concluded that this boy, whose essence you feel, will ask Sylvie to the high school prom." Cherise speaks in the same weird cadence as Madame Jakarta. They're two peas in a pod.

Madame Jakarta agrees that the music she "hears" must be from the Spring Fling band.

"I simply haven't had time to consult the Mercury table to determine precisely when Adam will ask her. That's why we came here. Can you tell us when he'll pop the question?" Cherise is clearly pleased at her engagement metaphor.

"Aha." Madame Jakarta nods vigorously. "I will focus on uncovering the truth behind your quest." Madame Jakarta releases my left wrist and snags my right palm with both her hands.

"The left hand is the hand we are born with," she explains. "The right hand indicates how circumstances have changed the path we travel." She bends low over my palm, so low I feel her breath on my fingers. All I can think about is when I'll get a chance to wash my hands.

Madame Jakarta looks at my right hand for a while, then unceremoniously drops it, snatching up my left hand again. She repeats this back-and-forth pattern a few times before declaring: "You have two love lines. One tapers off to friendship and another picks up where the first left off." She shows me the wrinkle in my palm that she claims is my second love line.

"Your journey began on one line, but you will not find completion until you have moved to the other." Madame Jakarta then announces, "It is time for your quest to commence."

The scent of the candle is making me light-headed and I want to get out of there as soon as humanly possible. "What does any of this have to do with Adam and the prom?" I ask, feeling totally exasperated.

"Everything," Madame Jakarta says. "Or perhaps nothing."

I've had enough psychic-speak. I have no idea what she's saying and I really don't care. It's nearly eight o'clock and my evening schedule's toast. The guys have been in the tea house so long I imagine they've floated down a chamomile river. I want to get out of there and salvage what little time I have left with Adam before nine o'clock. Plus, I still need to get next door to Wanda's to snag my sewing machine.

If Madame Jakarta isn't going to at least humor Cherise by answering her question and making up a date that Adam will ask me to the dance, then I don't want to stay any longer. What a waste of ten bucks! With escape firmly in mind, I pull super hard and finally manage to take back both my hands.

I pick myself up off the pillow and head toward the door. I don't turn around to see if Cherise is behind me. The clumping of her boots confirms that she's following.

"Sylvie." Madame Jakarta's sharp tone

stops me in my tracks. "If you are honest with yourself, you will forget the question and respond to the quest."

Yeah, yeah, yeah. Whatever that means. I get the message. Enough's enough. I'm done. I shove open the door and breathe in the cool, fresh air.

"And Cherise," Madame Jakarta says right before we've escaped, "it would serve you well to rethink your predictions."

Cherise nods as if she's seriously considering Madame Jakarta's admonition.

And finally, thankfully, blessedly, we're back out on Twelfth Avenue, free from Madame Jakarta's Psychic Shop.

Whew.

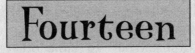

Fourteen

*Are you willing to let everyone know about
your romance? The stars say yes . . .
what do you say?*
www.astrology4stars.com

I've given up and decided to desert the
formality of a schedule, for a more free-flowing
attitude. Just a wee bit more free-flowing,
mind you. I can't handle much more than
that.

My decision has nothing to do with the
fact that Madame Jakarta told me to give up
my schedule. Nothing at all. I swear it on
my telescope. No matter how good my
intentions, the schedule wasn't working.

When Cherise arrives at my apartment

at 6:37 a.m. Friday morning, I immediately reconciled myself to the fact that yet another day was not going to go according to plan, so I simply gave up. As I now review the past week, I'm convinced the schedule really had no chance to work. It was a bad idea from the beginning.

I'm going to have to find another way to make sure I can still date Adam and keep up my grades. Rumor is the scholarship approval board is meeting next week—I read about it in a Yale chat room.

I'm eating waffles, silently staring at Jennifer and Tanisha's Elizabethan gown drawing, trying to decipher their notes on how the undergarment is to be sewn, when there's a knock on the door. Skipping inside the instant I open the door, Cherise drops her book bag in the foyer and fixes herself a bowl of our most nutritious cereal, Rice Krispies.

"Do you have any soy milk?" she asks as she rifles through our silverware drawer for a spoon.

"No," I tell her.

"Organic milk?"

"No!"

She grumbles for about three seconds

about the hormones in regular cow's milk, then decides to eat her cereal with vitamin-enriched orange juice instead. Gross. Cherise carries her bowl to the table and grabs herself a chair next to my father. It's early, but he's already dressed for work and he's wearing one of my favorite ties, with gold and blue specks. Hair combed and glasses pushed up, he looks like the serious businessman that he is, as he sits reading the newspaper.

"Madame Jakarta is a quack," Cherise tells me between cereal bites. I look over at my father. I assume that since he frequents Wanda's shop, he knows about Madame Jakarta, by name if not reputation. He's immersed in the business section of the *Cincinnati Enquirer*. I wonder if he's listening to us or not.

Apparently not, because he keeps his nose buried in his newspaper when Cherise says, "I finally checked the Mercury chart last night. Then I compared it to your astrological charts." Cherise takes another bite of her Krispies, chews, and swallows. "There is no way Madame Jakarta is right. About anything."

I'd agree if I could even remember one

single thing she said. I effectively washed away her words when I washed my hands after getting home. With antibacterial soap. "What exactly did Madame Jakarta say that she might have been right about?" I ask, wracking my brain for one morsel of last night's reading that might have had lasting relevance. "As far as I can recall, she said nothing interesting."

"She said that Adam wasn't your true love." Cherise polishes off her cereal, then tips the bowl to drink the remaining orange juice.

"She did?" I'm confused. "You'd think if she said something like that, I'd remember it."

"It was implied." Cherise is looking at me like I am a complete dope. "Weren't you listening?"

"I suppose not—and stop looking at me that way," I tell her. "I was too obsessed with the fact that she was breathing on my palms to have heard much of anything."

"Well." Cherise changes her expression. "That's what she said. And she's completely wrong. I've reviewed all my predictions and everything is still on track. Adam's definitely going to ask you to the prom and eventually, you're going to fall in love. I've no doubt that he's your diamond guy!"

"That's good news," I tell her, but don't mean it. While it's true that I'm seriously considering falling in love with Adam, I don't want it to be because we are still on some fated interplanetary path to happiness.

At the mention of my love life, I glanced at my father to gauge his reaction. Nothing. He doesn't even turn the newspaper page. For all I can tell, he's still reading.

Maybe Cherise and I should be having this conversation in another room.

Cherise barrels on before I can make the suggestion to move. "For the next few weeks, Mercury is going to be retrograde. That, combined with Neptune's moon path, confirms that Adam will ask you to the dance while you are at Gavin's party." She pauses. "Or maybe at the swim meet. This isn't an exact science, you know."

Really.

"What part about Mercury going retro means that he'll ask me?" I ask. Thing is, as much as I want to keep calling her predictions baloney, I'm willing to admit that I'm disappointed when they don't come true. When Adam asked me to the party instead of the dance, it warped the entire date. I don't want to be set up for another letdown.

"Retrograde, not retro," Cherise corrects me. "Retrograde means that the planet moves backward through the zodiac."

"Planets don't go backward," I tell her.

"Of course they don't!" She laughs. "Because of a shadow, they just sometimes look like they do." Silly me. I should have known. "When Mercury is retrograde some people make commitments they later regret." She warns me to be on the lookout for those sort of issues, then says, "But in your case, when the shadow falls over Mercury, what has been set in motion will come to be. Tomorrow's your night," she concludes.

"Great," I say, tapping down any feelings of anticipation I might have. I don't tell Cherise about how, at astronomy club, Adam had informed me that one of Neptune's moons was going to be high in the sky that night. I don't want her to get more excited. This is astrology, after all. The realist in me needs to keep her feet on the ground. There's still the chance—a big chance—that Adam won't ask me on Saturday night. Or ever.

"What if he doesn't ask?" With the dance two-and-a-half weeks away, I'm willing to give Cherise one more chance, but deal or no deal, at this point, I want a prom date and am going to take matters in my own hands soon.

Cherise gets up from the table, carries her bowl to the sink, rinses it, and puts it in the dishwasher before answering. "*If* he doesn't ask," she says as though there is no way he won't, "we'll take the universal risk." She points one finger at me. "You can ask him to the prom yourself on Sunday."

"Sunday," I confirm, relieved that this insanity is nearly over. One more day and I can ask Adam to the prom with Cherise's blessing. After that, if we do happen to fall in love, it'll be all about us and not because Saturn sits on Capricorn, or something like that.

For the first time in days, a decision about my love life has been made that I'm completely comfortable with. Cherise and I have a plan to get me to the dance. I like plans nearly as much as I like schedules.

Cherise goes downstairs to wait for me while I brush my teeth. I come back into the kitchen area where my father has put down his paper and removed his glasses.

"So," he says. "You're going to ask Adam to the prom." He was listening after all!

"Uh, yeah," I reply.

He doesn't say another word.

And neither do I.

Saturday morning. This afternoon, I'll be working at the tux shop up until my big second date with Adam but until then, I've got seven free hours to work on Jennifer's and Tanisha's costume designs. Ever since I woke up, I've been itching to get started. Before I even got out of bed I've been thinking about a way to alter the Elizabethan gown slightly to insure that Tanisha doesn't get her dancing shoes caught in the 100 percent organic cotton.

I've already finished my morning chores and reviewed my psych notes for Monday's quiz. Getting the must-do's out of the way was key. I can now focus on the wanna-dos: I wanna sew. I like the feel of the fabric slipping through my fingers. I love the vibration of the foot petal. The costume material has a clean and freshly ironed smell, which sticks with me long after I've walked away from the dresses.

Creating something beautiful is truly ful-filling. Sewing these costumes reminds me of when I made that wedding dress. I'm happy. Really happy.

I look at my watch again, Jennifer and Tanisha should be here by now. They prom-ised to come help and I, in turn, promised not to start without them. I'll wait for a little while.

Tick tock. Twenty minutes later, the Fashionistas still haven't arrived. Figuring their grace period is over, I decide to start without them. I sit down at my sewing machine and slide two carefully cut pieces of off-white cotton batiste under the needle. My bare foot is hovering over the foot pedal when . . .

The doorbell rings.

My father's already gone for the day. Saturdays are insane at the shop since most weddings and events take place on Saturday. You'd be surprised how many guys forget to rent their tuxes before an event and scramble for an open tux shop that can alter on the spot. My father's built a reputation for taking last-minute clients that no one else can help. Mornings aren't so bad, Dad can handle things alone, but by this afternoon, the shop will be a zoo. That's when I'll pitch in.

The doorbell buzzes a second time. I know the fabric isn't going anywhere, but the idea I had for the undergarment is stuck in my head and I want to complete the basting without breaking my concentration. It feels a bit like having to turn off a favorite TV show when the guests arrive for dinner.

One last look at the two batiste pieces to remind myself what I was planning and I hurry to the front door.

Jennifer and Tanisha are standing in the hallway, with Cherise.

"We brought an extra pair of hands," Jennifer tells me, her blond hair slicked back with a headband. She's wearing a sweatsuit. The low-rise boot-cut bottoms have swirls of rhinestones down the legs and the brand name printed across the butt. The jacket has a zipper with a cut crystal pull. It's a sweatsuit, but definitely not designed for sweating.

"We brought snacks." Tanisha explains how they ran into Cherise at the donut shop around the corner. Tanisha shoves a white paper bag in my hand.

I love donuts. They are the perfect food.

Sugar and grease—what's not to love? Being tall and thin, I've never counted calories, but if I did, I'd give up everything else before I stopped eating donuts.

Tanisha's black curls stand in stark contrast to the white T-shirt she is wearing with jeans. Unlike Jennifer, Tanisha doesn't need a designer name across her butt. Her whole being shouts, "I'm a goddess," even when she's super casual.

"When we told her we were coming here, Cherise offered to help for a while," Tanisha explains.

Yikes. I just know Cherise will immediately confiscate the spool of metallic thread I brought home from the tux shop. It's synthetic and comes from—*gasp*—the Amnesty International–offending country of Bangladesh. Problem is, I need that thread to attach the nymph's wings to Jennifer's gown.

I suppose I can work around the wings until Cherise leaves. I'd rather not chase away the assistance simply because I have contraband thread.

I welcome them all in and shut the apartment door. Then, I scoot ahead of the pack. I need to get to my room first so I can hide the thread. Sweeping into my room, I snag the small spool off the side table of my sewing machine and quickly stuff it into my jeans pocket.

I turn to the stacks of neatly folded fabric and paper patterns that are spread out on my table. And bed. And floor. I organized everything we would need to do today into three distinct piles. Within each stack, fabrics, threads, and patterns are sorted by design and color. I explain the system to my apprentices.

When I first agreed to sew the costumes (or Cherise agreed for me), Jennifer and Tanisha provided me with size-appropriate paper patterns for each of their designs. After I made a pattern for my own dress, I cut the material for all three. The patterns are still pinned to the individual fabric pieces.

Over the past couple of weeks, I've managed to nearly finish Jennifer's wood nymph. I left some parts loosely sewed with large stitches so that after she tries it on, I can make the necessary adjustments.

Tanisha's costume is less complete. I explain to Tanisha the change I wanted to make: a hidden slit in the undergarment skirt, so she doesn't trip over herself while dancing. "Awesome!" She beams at me for my quick thinking and seamstress know-how. The praise feels good. For the first time since Cherise announced that Mars entered Gemini, I am content.

Like a queen bee, I set everyone to task. Jennifer's slipping into her costume. Tanisha's laying out the pieces of her gown and matching threads for each fabric. And Cherise's getting a start on my Cinderella costume. Not having a date to the dance, I have put that costume on the back burner. I cut the fabric but haven't done anything else. Cherise's going to pin the material for stitching.

With donuts to fuel us, and music from Jennifer's MP3 player filling the air, we are off and running. Even without a schedule, or perhaps because I ditched the schedule, it's shaping up to be a terrific day.

Fifteen

Now is the time to zero in on what you want.
Stay focused.
www.astrology4stars.com

I went to work ready for the swim meet and my second official date with Adam. I was overdressed at work and feel totally over-dressed for the swim meet, as well. While we were working on the costumes, Jennifer and Tanisha decided that I needed a makeover. Jennifer took a break to rush home and get me some of her clothes. Tanisha did my hair and then they worked together on my makeup.

Cherise was thrilled. She said that the borrowed clothing would help me feel sexy, which would make me even more open to falling in love. She was so determined that I dress up tonight that she didn't even check the clothing labels for manufacturing information; instead just told me to put them on. Of course, she did insist that they use her organic, non-animal tested, botanical makeup for my sexy look.

So here I am, wearing a shorter-than-ever dark skirt, black opaque tights, and a maroon camisole covered with sparkly beads. I have a denim jacket with black and maroon appliquéd flowers to "pull the outfit together."

Standing in the latest peep-toe heels poolside seems absurd. I'm completely obsessed with the possibility that I might tip over and end up in the pool. I don't quite get why every other girl doesn't seem as worried as I am. They're all dressed like me. I fit right in.

And yet, I don't. At every turn, I'm reminded that this is Adam's turf, not mine. The kids I normally see at school aren't here, with the exception of Jennifer and Tanisha. They are nice to me as ever, but they also have their own social group to attend to. I'm spending a great deal of time alone.

To compensate for my discomfort, I focus on the swimming.

Adam's such a great swimmer and the sight of him in that little, bitty swimsuit, well, if this were the 1800s, I'd have fainted dead away. They'd have needed smelling salts to revive me. I've felt his muscles beneath his shirt, but imagination pales to the real thing.

Easily winning his four races, Adam helps bring our school's swim team to victory. I'm cheering so loudly, my throat hurts.

After his final race, Adam comes over to me in the stands and hands me his goggles before rushing off to get a towel. How romantic is that? Holding those blue plastic goggles, my heart leaps into my throat and lodges there. It is amazing.

Jennifer says that Adam will definitely ask me to the Spring Fling at Gavin's party. She also reminds me that she and Tanisha aren't going to be there. It's Jennifer's mom's birthday, so they are headed to a surprise party for her instead.

Now, it'll be just me and Adam, and Gavin at the party. Oh joy. I wish Cherise was going to be there. Or Nathan. Or even Tyler, for pity's sake. Someone I'm friendly with. Anyone.

I can do this. I tell myself that over and over during the car ride to the party. I can be social. I will have a great time. I'll talk to people I might not otherwise spend time with and enjoy myself.

I'm going to this party not just to be with Adam, but to prove that I can fit into his world as smoothly as he seems to fit into mine. Oh, and I'm crossing my fingers that he's going to ask me to prom. Tonight is my night.

While they were dressing me up, Tanisha, Jennifer, and Cherise came up with a plan to go to the costume store on Monday evening with their dates. Whether Adam asks me tonight or I ask him tomorrow, we're set to go to the costume store with them. The thought of wearing Jennifer and Tanisha's Cinderella dress with my own Prince Charming is so awesome, I have to hold myself back from asking Adam to prom right here in the car.

As he drives, I find that I'm actually looking forward to the party. I can do this. I really can.

I wish I wasn't obsessed with dental hygiene, but along with my love for the stars, this was another "gift" from my mom.

She made me brush twice a day and floss every night. What other one-year-old has her own box of floss? I had two teeth and was already looking for food caught between them.

When we get to the party, I decide that a quick check in the mirror is a good idea. If I'm going to peel myself out of my shell and be social, I need to feel my most confident. Even though I haven't eaten anything since leaving the apartment, a tooth check and a little more lip gloss will be just the security blanket I need.

"I'm going to find the rest room," I tell Adam as he takes my jacket and ushers me into Gavin Masterson's party.

"I'll get us some drinks," Adam says, wandering off into the crowd.

The house is packed. It crosses my mind to wonder if Gavin's parents know that there are hundreds of high school students crammed into every corner of their lovely home. Then I hear the crash of breaking glass from the living room and my fear is confirmed: His parents have no clue.

I wander upstairs looking for a bathroom. I run into a group of girls who I don't know. They're shouting my name and hugging me like we're all best friends. They're gushing, reviewing the moment when Adam handed me the victory goggles.

"Such an awesome swimmer," one girl tells me.

"And so hot," another says.

I look for an excuse to disappear while they go on and on about how lucky I am to be at the party with Adam. After a few minutes of them goo-ing all over me, I find a place to slip in the word "thanks," as if I'm somehow responsible for Adam's magnificent performance at the swim meet, and then rush off, still looking for a mirror.

This whole fitting-in-with-the-popular-group thing is harder than I expected. I'll take five in the bathroom to regroup, then go find Adam. After a while, maybe I'll try again with the gushing girls. I'm hoping there's more to them than blond hair and belly button rings. It's going to be my personal mission to find out what.

While I stand outside the bathroom waiting my turn, a swimmer pal of Adam's comes and presses an envelope into my hands.

"Is it from Adam?" I ask, my curiosity piqued. I don't even know my delivery boy's name. I think it might be John or James.

"Nah. Some guy outside gave me twenty dollars to find you," he tells me.

The bathroom door opens and even though I'm next in line, I let a girl go in before me. This feels a bit spooky. "Do you know who the guy was?" I ask my messenger.

"I think he goes to our school, but I'm not sure," the guy answers with a shrug. "I didn't see nothin' but the cash in his hand." Good thing a crime wasn't committed. This kid would be a terrible witness. Having earned his money, my delivery boy disappears down the stairs back into the party.

I quickly rip open the envelope. It's an invitation. To a bar.

My initial thought is that I'm not old enough to go to a bar. And unlike many kids at school, I don't have a fake ID. As I'm thinking this, I see the handwritten note at the bottom of the invitation. In neatly printed blue letters it reads:

Wristbands will be given to those over the age of 21.

I note the facts: next Friday night. Eight p.m. A bar called the Holy Grail in a trendy part of Cincinnati called Pleasant Ridge.

The question is, who wrote it and why? It's bizarre and I'm a little scared. This is the stuff Hitchcock movies are made of.

If you think that going to a party at Gavin's is out of character for me, there's no way I'll be going to some bar in Pleasant Ridge by myself next weekend. No chance in hell. When I finally get into the bathroom, I tear up the invitation and throw away the pieces in the trash can. With a quick check of my teeth, I put on my lip gloss, tell myself, "I can do this" one final time, and go back out to the party.

Adam is standing by the fireplace in the living room talking to Gavin. Whatever glass object I heard break had been cleaned up while I was away. "You were gone a while," he says. "Everything all right?"

"I'm fine," I tell him, struggling to put the mysterious invitation out of my mind and turn my focus to having a good time with my boyfriend. "It's just so crowded it's hard to get around."

Adam looks down at my leg. "Your ankle okay?" I feel a shot of color hit my checks. He's so sweet that he still cares about my ankle! No one else ever bothers to ask.

"Fine," I repeat, gesturing toward Gavin. "Sorry I interrupted."

Gavin's bleached-blond hair twinkles in the room's overhead lighting. In elementary school, he was a brunette, then suddenly in seventh grade he became a poster boy for the Big Island of Hawaii. Too bad we live in Ohio.

"How's it going, Gavin?" I ask as cheerily as I can.

"Night just got better," Gavin replies with a flirtatious wink.

"Sylvie's *my* girl," Adam tells Gavin, giving him a friendly punch in the gut. "Get your own." Adam puts his arm around me possessively.

"But I like yours," Gavin replies and the two of them laugh.

I'm not sure whether to laugh, too, or not. I've never been the subject of guy talk before, at least not while I was present. I don't know how to react. I just stand there wondering if I should be flattered or repulsed as the two of them pretend to fight over who gets me.

The subject switches to the results of tonight's swim meet. After a few minutes, I put my hand on Adam's arm. I'm not sure how else to send the message that I no longer want to be standing here with Gavin and that I'd like for us to move on. Those giggling girls are nearby. We could go talk to them instead. See how that goes.

Adam doesn't catch my clue. Briefly pausing his conversation with Gavin, Adam hands me a cup of red-colored punch that was sitting on the fireplace mantel, saying, "Oh, I got you some punch."

"Thanks." I take a sip. Not only is it spiked, but it's so sweet, I cough.

Adam downs his drink in one gulp, hands me the keys to his car, and says, "You're the designated driver tonight. I'm getting a beer. Want some more punch?" I look at him sideways. Clearly Adam doesn't know the punch is spiked.

"No, thanks," I reply, setting my drink on the mantel and putting his keys in my purse.

Adam leans in and gives my earlobe a nibble. He whispers, "Now's your chance to patch things up with Gavin. I'll be back in a few minutes. Be nice," he breathes in my ear before wandering off in the direction of the nearest keg.

Because Adam asked, I'm going to try

my best to be nice. But only because Adam asked. "You swam really well tonight," I say, unable to think of anything else.

Gavin accepts my praise, then asks, "Where's your buddy, Cherise, tonight?"

"Not here," I say simply. Keeping the conversation to the basics seems like the way to go.

"I thought the two of you are stuck together like glue." There's a look on Gavin's face that I don't like. I avoid his gaze.

"She's my friend," I tell him. "But we aren't stuck together." What is Gavin up to? He's making it hard to be nice. . . .

"I've never liked her," Gavin tosses in as if I asked what he thinks.

"I don't really care what you—," I begin, feeling a surge of emotion rising to the surface. Suddenly, I'm back in fourth grade. Once a bully, always a bully.

I take a deep breath and reframe my response. "You don't have to like her," I say hoping that will end the conversation. "I honestly don't care." There. How was that?

Adam wants me to be nice. For Cherise's honor, I should argue or kick him in the knee. I'm not going to do either. Tonight, I'm trying to be neutral, like Switzerland.

I look around for the nearest exit. The front door's in sight, over Gavin's right shoulder, about thirty feet away. I'll grab Adam on the way out. I'm certain he'll understand.

"Have you ever wondered why I stole from Cherise in fourth grade and not from you, Sylvie?" Gavin flashes a wicked grin and steps in closer to me, blocking my view of the front door. "Because I liked you. Cherise's too weird, always has been, but you . . ." He's looking down at me with a hungry expression. "I've always had a soft place in my heart for you." My discomfort is growing. "Did you know the swim team's all about sharing? We share lockers and towels." He raises his eyebrows as he adds, "All kinds of things."

Gavin wobbles as he bends closer to me. I can smell the alcohol on his breath. Steadying himself, he drapes an arm over my shoulder, saying, "You could tutor me in math and I could tutor you in . . ." He whispers a word that I have never considered saying aloud.

I try to pull away but he holds me tighter under his arm, pulling me firmly against his side. The hand over my shoulder is now slowly creeping across my shirt. When Adam told me to be nice to him, I don't imagine that letting Gavin cop a feel was what my boyfriend had in mind.

I'm about to knee Gavin in the crotch, just like I saw on a self-defense program on TV, when Adam reappears, beer in hand. Gavin straightens up and pulls back his hand, but doesn't let me go entirely.

Adam takes one look at the way Gavin's arm is wrapped around my shoulder and says, "I'm so glad you two are finally getting along." Adam beams at me. "See? I told you this was a great idea. I knew you could work it out." Then, very sincerely, he says, "Thanks, Sylvie. I really appreciate your effort." And as if his thanks weren't enough, he adds, "My best girl and my best friend are finally on good terms!" Adam looks like a kid who has just gotten the gift he always wanted, a truce between . . . Wait a second—His what?! His best friend??

Adam's glowing like this reconciliation is somehow better than world peace. How am I supposed to tell him I hate Gavin more than ever? I tried to be nice, but his "best friend" came on to me. His best friend is a complete jerk and—

I can't tell him. Somehow, despite my warning, Adam and Gavin became friends. Good friends.

There's nothing I can think to do or say, so I simply paste a frozen smile on my lips. It's painful.

Removing his arm from around me, Gavin tells Adam, "Sylvie and I were talking about sharing."

"That's great!" Adam cheers, then drapes his arm around me in the way that Gavin's arm just was. "Swim team is all about sharing."

"Exactly." Gavin smiles wolfishly at Adam and then, when he thinks Adam isn't looking, winks at me. "That's exactly what I told Sylvie," he says to Adam while staring at me.

I'm feeling sick. Will someone remind me why I came to this dumb party? When I'm at school, wearing my own clothes and surrounded by people of my choosing, I have a certain level of confidence. In the name of Yale, I've turned down a few come-ons. But here, I'm so out of my element that I can't even figure out how to respond to a guy like Gavin. I let him treat me poorly and that feels rotten. Even knowing that I did it for Adam still feels icky, especially since I told Adam how much I don't like Gavin and what he's all about.

I should have kicked Gavin in the balls when he first bullied Cherise back in fourth grade. I missed my opportunity then, and I missed it again tonight.

Now I am ready for Adam to get the message that I want to leave loud and clear. No hand on the arm for me. This time, I really want to leave and I'm going to be direct about it. "Let's get some air," I say firmly. I want to get away from Gavin as quickly as I can.

"Okay." Adam sets the rest of his beer up on the fireplace, next to my unfinished drink, and takes my hand in his.

"Outside, huh?" Gavin asks with a tone that implies that we are about to have sex on the front lawn. And then there's that look that tells me that when I'm done having sex with Adam, Gavin would be interested if I want to come back inside for his turn. "Have fun," he adds, looking only at me.

"Oh, we will," Adam says obviously responding to the innuendo, without noticing Gavin's lecherous look. He takes my hand and leads me outside.

I take in the night air and try to forget about what happened with Gavin. It's not Adam's fault his friend is such a pig. Gavin has multiple personalities: the cool, jock, swim captain and the evil, lunch money–stealing, girlfriend-grabbing, slimeball. I wish Adam could see Gavin for who he really is.

Another deep breath and I feel soothed. I'm back under the stars, where I feel most comfortable.

"I'm glad you came with me tonight," Adam says, gently pushing a strand of hair off my face and tucking it behind my ear. "I know this isn't your crowd, so I want you to know how grateful I am."

His words, and the way he's looking at me, give me the resolve I need to shove aside Gavin's nasty come-on. It's just me and Adam now. The way it should be.

He's going to ask me to prom. Finally. I know it.

"Will you go to the Spring Fling Prom with me?" he asks without any preamble. I don't even pretend to be surprised. I immediately say yes.

I tell him about the costume store and Adam agrees to come along on Monday after swim practice. Then he kisses me to seal the date. We make out for a little while, then feeling exhausted by the whole Gavin thing and the fact that I really don't want to stay at the party, I tell Adam I want to go home.

It's early, not even midnight yet. Since Adam isn't drunk, I give him back his keys and ask him to get me my coat. "I'll wait here," I tell him. I'm pretty sure he'll go back to the party after driving me home. Adam doesn't say it, but I get that vibe.

We kiss one more time on the steps leading up to my building. I allow my lips to slide slightly open. Adam urges my mouth a little wider, teasing my tongue with his.

I'm going to prom with an amazing guy. He likes math and science and astronomy. He's going to be a doctor and is an academic overachiever. He can be social with anyone, fits in with everyone. He likes my friends, my father, and most important, me. If I believed in astrology, I'd have to agree with Cherise that Adam's my diamond guy. It's as if he was made just for me.

So why is it that our kisses are never intense or magical or thrilling or amazing? Not that I'm a kissing expert, but something is missing. What can it be?

Sixteen

Expect the unexpected.
www.astrology4stars.com

I'm so confused, I can't sleep.

It's one in the morning. After tossing and turning for hours, I've given up. Grabbing my telescope, I tiptoe past my father's bedroom door and sneak up to the roof to talk to my mom. I do that sometimes when I feel like I need a little advice.

The stairs to the roof are between my apartment and the hall-mounted fire extinguisher. In case there's a fire and people have to get out of the apartment building quickly, the door's always unlocked, so I'm not surprised to discover it's already slightly ajar. Someone must have come up to tan earlier and not shut the door all the way.

As I set up my Hartforde telescope, I'm so deep in thought that when I hear my name softly spoken, I nearly jump out of my skin.

"Sylvie?" It's Tyler.

I'm so freaked out that I stumble backward. My foot catches the tripod for my telescope and suddenly, the world begins to look as if it's gone "retrograde," appearing to move in slow motion.

I'm falling backward, down toward the hard asphalt of the roof. My body rotates slightly as I tumble. I'm going to scrape my knee for sure. Or my hands, if I try to catch myself. Or maybe both.

My telescope is tilting the other direction, too far for me to reach. Lens first, it's moving toward the ground. I know with every fiber in my being that the flip-mirror will shatter. I can't possibly afford to get a replacement part. Not to mention that whole broken mirror = seven years bad luck stuff. I can't afford that either.

All this crosses my brain in the few seconds since Tyler startled me.

Tyler.

I look at up him, horrified and expectant. He appears confused. With psychic clarity (Madame Jakarta would be proud) I *know* what he's thinking. Tyler's considering that he has about a millisecond to make a choice and act. Should he save me or save my telescope? What will he do?

A flick of his wrist and Tyler's black Zorro cloak is suddenly soaring toward me. His body flings the other way toward my Hartforde. His plan is obvious. I'm supposed to land softly on the cloak, while he snags my precious telescope mid-descent. Tyler Gregory, Man in Black, is attempting to save the day.

Unfortunately, his cloak lands over my head instead of under my hands.

"Ouch." I grimace as my left hip takes the brunt of the fall. At least I didn't scrape up my hands or knee. But there will be a bruise, a big, juicy, black-and-blue one. I can't check out the damage to my leg though, because the cloak is over my head. And even if it wasn't cutting off my vision, I have my eyes closed bracing for the crashing sound of my telescope smashing against the hard rooftop into a gazillion little pieces.

Nothing. Silence.

Then Tyler, "Sylvie?! You all right?"

He pulls the cloak off my head, draping it carefully around my shoulders, to keep me . . . warm . . . or safe. Suddenly I'm overwhelmed by the scent of him in the fabric. It's that woodsy, earthy scent I noticed in the café. Kind of a strange thing to keep noticing, but then again my sense of scent must be enhanced because my eyes are still shut tight.

"Telescope?" I grind out the one word, slowly opening my right eye.

"No damage," he replies, but there's an edge to his voice. "Wish I could say the same for you."

I open both eyes fully and allow Tyler to help me up off the hard rooftop. We both look down at my thigh. Even in the moonlight, it's clear that there's a growing red patch that will be blue by dawn. My first assessment was correct, however: no blood. Too bad I hadn't thought to change out of my cotton sleep shorts and tank top before I came up here. If I'd been wearing jeans, I'd have had a more durable, slightly thicker padding.

"You tried to save me." I thank Tyler, handing him his cloak and taking a large step back, widening the distance between us. I gotta get away from his scent. It's making my heart race in uncomfortable ways. I'm certain I'm having an allergic reaction to his cologne. At least that's what I tell myself. Over and over again.

For every step I'm taking backward, he's taking one forward, hand outstretched. It's just as I begin to get a bit nervous, wondering why he won't take a hint and let the distance between us grow, that I notice Tyler is holding out my telescope.

I stop running the backward marathon. I thank him profusely. From the bottom of my heart. I take the telescope and clutch it to my chest, like a new mother coddles her baby. "You made the right choice diving for the telescope," I tell him.

"I thought you might say that." Tyler grins, his white (very white, I respectfully admire) teeth shining in the moonlight. He shrugs. "Still wish my plan would've worked. I could have rescued the damsel and her telescope in one swift movement."

"You tried and that's what counts." I set the telescope back on the tripod's three legs, and angle the lens toward the night sky. "You might dress like Batman," I say with a giggle, "but you're only Bruce Wayne."

Tyler laughs. I like the way the sound echoes in the dark.

"What are you doing up here?" we ask each other at nearly the exact same time.

I decide to answer first and honestly, though I don't know what has possessed me to be so frank. "I came to talk to my mom," I tell him and point at the telescope. You'd think Tyler would pin me with one wide eye and say, "Huh?' or grab his cell phone and call 911 to have me committed to a psych ward, but he does neither. Tyler casually replies, "Say hi for me." And flashes me another toothy grin.

"Now your turn," I say simply.

He points across the rooftop to a place in the shadows. I now notice a sleeping bag laid out and a pillow.

"I was just about to settle in for the night," he says.

"You're sleeping up here?' I ask, stunned. "Isn't the rooftop uncomfortable?"

"I have an air mattress under my bag," he replies simply.

"Did you have a fight with your parents? Or Cherise?" I am wracking my brain trying to come up with a reason Tyler would want to sleep up here instead of in his room. I mean, I know why I like to sleep outside (not that I've ever slept on the roof of our apartment building before): Sleeping under the stars is a natural extension of my love for astronomy. As far as I know, Tyler doesn't love astronomy . . . so maybe he likes astrology?

He shakes his head at me. "Why do you think I'd have to be in a fight with someone to come out here? Couldn't it be that I just like sleeping under the stars?"

I shrug. "It just seems odd. You aren't in the astronomy club." I pause then ask, "Are you into astrology like Cherise?"

"No," Tyler answers. "Rest your brain, Sylvie. I like looking at the stars. It's nice to sleep under them. That's all there is to it."

I think about his answer. I guess I've never really considered that there's a middle ground between astronomy and astrology. I suppose Tyler's like most people: They like the stars because they're beautiful. They don't *need* to know about Neptune's moons. Or about "Neptune's moon" either.

I nod as I take in this new realization.

"Thanks," I tell Tyler.

"For what?"

I consider telling him that his perspective on the stars is intriguing or that because of his questions that day at the Corner Café, I now understand clearly why I want to study astronomy, but decide against it. "Just thanks," I reply. It's enough.

"You're welcome." He doesn't press me for more.

"Want to look through my telescope?" I ask him, then immediately wish I hadn't offered. It was a step backward. I actually like that Tyler's enjoying the stars simply because they twinkle. I don't want to mess with that.

I don't have to rescind my offer because Tyler turns me down. He moves across the roof and lies back on his sleeping bag, hands behind his head. "Want to look at the sky from my vantage?" he offers.

"I . . ." I nearly choke as I brush away the thought of lying down on an air mattress with Tyler. "No, thanks." I adjust the lens on my Hartforde and peer through the eyepiece.

I get lost in the stars and we're both silent for a while. It's comfortable. There's no need to fill the silence with words. I take a peek at Mercury, and laugh at the idea that all of Cherise's predictions will be coming true because it's "retrograde."

Time passes quickly. Tyler's still and quiet. I glance at him lying on his mattress under the glow of the moon and wonder if he's fallen asleep. I hope so, because I should go inside soon and I haven't talked to Mom yet. I decide to go ahead and speak out loud, like I usually do, pushing Tyler's presence out of my mind.

"Do you believe in destiny?" I ask in a low tone, my words drifting off the roof and floating upwards to Mom.

It's not like I really expect a female booming voice to say, "Relax, Sylvie. Enjoy the process of falling in love. Those kisses will get better because Adam is the guy for you!" or alternately, "If the relationship doesn't feel right, you should stop forcing it."

I look through the telescope lens, searching the skies for a sign that Mom has heard me. A shooting star or a little twinkle would be plenty reassuring. The sky seems still and quiet when I take a deep breath and ask my follow-up question on a long sigh. "What should I do?"

"Make your own destiny." The voice is so soft that at first I wonder if Mom has actually spoken to me from deep space. It takes a second to register; the voice, so smooth now, is the same one that surprised me when I first came to the rooftop.

"Tyler?" I ask, turning my head to face him.

"I know I'm interrupting a very private conversation, but I can't help myself." He rolls on his side and props himself up on one arm. I feel the heat of his gaze.

"It's okay. But what do you mean?" I pull myself back from the telescope and turn to face him straight on. "Make your own destiny?" I'm curious.

"The stars illuminate our path," Tyler says. "Like they have always done for explorers and navigators, the stars show us the way. Following the stars can provide courage to press forward when we feel lost." He pauses, then adds, "They can't tell us when or how to behave."

"I don't expect the stars to tell me exactly what to do," I say, feeling a bit judged.

When Tyler doesn't immediately respond, I put aside my initial reaction and allow myself to slip into that gray area where Tyler resides, the place where astronomy and astrology are secondary to the mysterious beauty of the sky. I look up and out at the night sky and imagine early explorers searching for the North Star to show them the way home.

They'd get lost, lose hope, and then, as Tyler said, look to the stars to show them the way through the ocean, across the forest, over the mountains. They didn't need to know how many planets were in our solar system, or the chemical makeup of cosmic debris, they only needed to find one big twinkling bulb in the sky, mark down its position from where it was the night before, and bravely march onward into previously uncharted territory. The stars were a guide. The path, their own.

"You always seem so calm and collected," I say, considering Tyler's words. "When do you ever need a bump in courage?"

He laughs then says, "Oh, Sylvie, you'd be surprised." His laughter fades away and Tyler slips over onto his back, looking up at the sky again. "Have you ever gone somewhere and done something completely out of character? Taken a huge risk with the hope that everything will turn out in your favor?"

I think about the past few hours. I went to a party at Gavin Masterson's, wore a mini-miniskirt, and was entirely out of my element, all because I wanted Adam to ask me to the prom.

"Yes," I say. "I did all that tonight."

Tyler doesn't reply. In fact, he's quiet so long I'm convinced that this time, he's really fallen asleep. In the quietude, I pack up my telescope. It's time for me to go inside and get to bed.

I start to slip toward the apartment building door, moving slowly so as not to wake Tyler up. As I open the door, I hear Tyler's whispered voice from behind me.

"Yeah. I did all that tonight, too."

Seventeen

*Look beyond the obvious. Let your mind's
eye bear witness to the world.*
www.astrology4stars.com

Costume Castle is not really a castle, no
matter what the name says. It's actually a
converted storefront in a strip mall. They
try to make it look all castle-y with an arch-
ing door frame and crenellations, but once
you're through the door, if you look back,
you can see that the gray bricks are nothing
but foam.

Adam picks me up at the tuxedo shop
after his swim practice. He waits until we're
at his car before sweeping me into his arms
and kissing me hard on the lips. "I've been

wanting to do that all day," he tells me as we break apart and get into the car. "There's no privacy in high school," he adds with a laugh.

"Me, too," I lie. How bad is it to pretend to your boyfriend that you've been dreaming about kissing him, when really the thought never crossed your mind? It was a busy day at school and as far as that Yale chat room is concerned, this is the week that scholarships will be announced. I've had a lot on my mind today.

As for the kiss, this one was too rough and quick to place on the rating scale. I am certain the knock-my-socks-off kiss is coming around the corner. I mean, it has to be, right?

We're all here. The quadruple date. Cherise and Nathan want to start in the medical aisle. They already borrowed surgical scrubs from Nathan's dad, a general surgeon. "We're looking for medical supplies," Cherise tells me as they head off together. "Let's meet back here in ten."

"Great," I say. I'm holding hands with Adam. I'd like to let go; my palm is getting a bit sweaty, but since he is making no move to break the hold, I'm not going to be the big killjoy.

Jennifer is going to the Spring Fling with her longtime boyfriend, Jordan Berman. Jordan's exactly the kind of guy you'd imagine dating a girl like Jennifer. Blond hair, blue eyes; Jordan's the ultimate jock. He plays three sports and excels at them all. I've actually never had a conversation with Jordan. We've never been in the same class and the only sports I've done at school were forced upon me by the PE requirement for graduation.

Now would be a perfect op for me to drop Adam's hand and give a half-wave "hello" to Jordan. But I don't. I nod and say, "Hey," instead. And then greet Lee, Tanisha's boyfriend, the same way.

Tanisha hasn't been dating Lee Cooke very long, but she's totally into him. Unlike Jennifer and Jordan, who look as good together as Angelina and Brad, Tanisha's choice of Lee baffles me. She's so good looking and Lee, well, let's just say, he isn't.

Since our freshman year, Lee and I have taken a lot of classes together. He's about three inches shorter than Tanisha, and round. Some might politely say he's "full." Not fat. His dark brown skin is stretched full of Lee Cooke. What he lacks in good looks, he more than makes up for in smarts. He's a genius. I swear. I do well in school because I work hard. Lee breezes through everything. In fact, though he's a senior like me, he's only sixteen because of all those grades he skipped in elementary school. I'm just glad that he decided to accept early admission to MIT for biochemistry. If he'd selected Yale, I'd have had to compete with him for one of those science scholarships. Not that I wouldn't win it, mind you, but it would be a bloody battle.

Jordan, Lee, and Adam all need costumes. Jordan needs to find something to complement Jennifer's wood nymph. Jennifer warned us that he'd like to be a tree. Tanisha and I are supposed to discourage him and point him to the male fairy-looking costumes instead. Personally, I think a tree is far more manly, but Jennifer does not want to be dancing with an oak.

Lee will go Renaissance. I shiver at the thought of seeing him in tights and a codpiece.

Adam pulls on our attached hands and leads me to the prince outfits. He finally lets go of my hand to take a royal purple velvet cape off a rack. I quickly shove my free hands into my blue jeans pockets. What's the matter with me? I like holding hands with Adam! I shouldn't be hiding my palms, I should be grabbing his hand back in mine and begging him not to let go. But I'm not. I push my hands down into my pockets as far as they can go.

Adam selects a few things to try on and we meet Cherise, Jennifer, Tanisha, Nathan, Jordan, and Lee by the dressing rooms.

Obviously Jordan convinced Jennifer that a fairy costume was going too far for an athlete like himself. He's wearing a tree. It has branches and leaves and an owl hole for his head. I am struggling so hard to hold in my laughter that I nearly choke.

Lee looks equally ridiculous. Like Romeo, only fuller. He is wearing bright green ballooning pantaloons with beige tights. I have to look away from the cod-piece, which is like an old-fashioned support cup, worn on the outside of a man's tights. My eyes are drawn to it every time I glance in Lee's direction. I force myself to look away. Tanisha says something about how she thinks Lee would look better as a red Romeo and hustles back to the aisle where they found his costume. He retreats into the dressing room to wait for Tanisha to come back.

Cherise and Nathan found their costumes. They would have preferred stethoscopes made of recycled rubber tubing, but compromised on plastic ones made in the USA (where we have strong child labor laws) instead. After one look at Lee in his codpiece, they decided not to wait around. It might take a while for Tanisha to find the right outfit for Lee, so they go to pay. We'll meet them at the deli next door when we're done.

"Adam?" I call out. He's been in the dressing room quite a while. "Need any help?"

A throaty laugh is his reply.

"What's taking so long?" I ask.

"Tights," is his response.

I smile. Girls are used to pulling on tights. Maybe I should have told Adam to roll down to the foot before shoving his whole leg into the tights. Then again, live and learn.

A few minutes later the door to Adam's dressing room opens. It's like one of those scenes in the teen movies, where the music starts to play and the room fills with smoke. The handsome hero emerges in soft light.

Jennifer is standing next to me. Hearing Adam's voice outside the dressing room, Tanisha comes rushing down the aisle to get a look. When she sees him, she nearly drops the armful of costumes she is carrying.

"So?" Adam puts out his arms and spins around for us to see the whole costume. He's wearing tights, all right. Bright blue tights. Red cape, blue breastplate, yellow belt. "Check this out. It was hanging in the dressing room." He turns around again. "It fits just right."

I have to admit that unlike Lee, Adam looks hot in tights, but this is not the costume I imagined.

"I thought you were going to be Prince Charming." Jennifer is saying what I'm thinking. "Sylvie has been sewing herself a Cinderella dress."

"The whole Prince Charming thing just isn't me." Adam adjusts his breastplate, centering the big *S* on his chest. "I'm a little sick of the whole PC nickname around school. I think this costume will help destroy that image."

I thought the PC thing was funny. It's part of why I agreed to make the Cinderella costume for myself. This is such a bummer.

"You look great," I say honestly, because he does. Then I think, If Adam's going to wear that to the dance, do I have to change costumes, too? Is there even such a thing as a Lois Lane costume?

Truth is, I've barely started to sew the Cinderella dress. I've been too busy with the nymph and gown. I remind myself that I've set aside tomorrow night to make headway. There's still plenty of time to get it done. I love the dress that Jennifer and Tanisha designed. I really don't want to change costumes.

Adam's being super sweet, but I can tell he really wants to be Superman. I can compromise. "We'll call me a damsel-in-distress instead of Cinderella."

"Terrific!" Adam cheers. "I'll save you!" He raises his eyebrows and grins, adding, "As many times as you'd like."

I smile, but it's strained. I need a little while to process the change. I'll be okay. I mean, I did sorta force the whole PC thing on him in the first place. I never considered that Adam might want to pick his own costume.

Superman and a damsel-in-distress. Okay. And, there are those tights. . . .

Adam goes back to the dressing room to change into his regular clothes.

Tanisha finally finds a costume for Lee. He's wearing regular pants tied with a rope belt. A peasant shirt and leather vest. More plebian than royalty, but it's a far cry from the tights and codpiece. Thank goodness. Let's leave the tights to Adam.

If we need comic relief on prom night, Jordan will provide it. Jennifer couldn't change his mind. He's getting the tree.

We're set to go.

Before we pay, Adam suggests that I go pick out a crown to complete my own damsel costume. I'm not sure I need a crown now, but Adam insists. "Okay." I agree to go find myself a crown while he gets in line for a cashier.

I wander over to where we found the prince capes. There's a shelf full of crowns and a mirror on the side of the aisle. I pick out two and carry them to the mirror. One is more of a tiara than a full crown. I set it on my head. Tanisha offered to sweep my hair into an updo, whatever that means. I think the tiara will be a better choice than the bigger crown, and it's three dollars less, so, decision made, I walk back to put the crown away.

I stop.

Something has caught my eye and I can't seem to move. I hear Adam calling my name from the front of the store, but don't immediately respond.

I'm standing in front of a costume display, frozen to the floor, heart racing. I don't understand what is going on inside me. I mean, why am I staring at this particular rack? What does it mean?

I don't need a black cloak.

Do I?

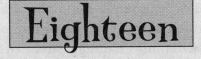

Eighteen

Time for action.
www.astrology4stars.com

The week flew by and although I have been
checking the mail and my e-mail daily,
there's no word from the scholarship committee. Not yet. It's Friday and today's mail
had nothing with that famous Yale crest in
the left-hand corner. Maybe tomorrow.

Now I'm getting dressed. Casual. My
own clothes. Blue jeans, black tank top,
cute boots, funky long coat. I bought the
coat last year, but haven't had many occasions to wear it. It's that funky. It looks
solid grassy green from a distance, but when
you get close there are autumn-colored

flecks in the material. It's a "going out" coat and tonight . . . I'm going out.

But not with Adam.

I know you're probably wondering where my boyfriend is. Well, I suppose you could say he gave me the night off. Adam wanted to go to the movies with some guys from swimming. He suggested that I take the evening and focus on sewing the dresses since the prom is only eight days away.

"Great idea," I told him.

I lied.

There *is* a lot of work to be done on the dresses, that part is true, but I'm not planning to do it tonight. Nope. I'm wearing my kick-ass jacket and going to a bar. Eight p.m. The Holy Grail.

I never told Cherise about the cryptic invitation I was given at Gavin Masterson's house. I never told a soul. This is my secret. Mine alone.

I might not have gone tonight if Adam had wanted to do something together. But the truth is, I was glad for the reprieve. Who needs a break from their boyfriend? Me, apparently.

As I sit on the bus to Pleasant Ridge, the butterflies in my stomach begin to multiply. I'm a bit nauseated.

I actually like taking public transportation in Cincinnati. We have those new buses that use old cooking grease for fuel, which makes them smell vaguely like French fries. Under normal circumstances the smell is appealing, but tonight, my stomach is churning and I long for the old smell of gasoline and burning oil.

When I get off the bus a few blocks away from the club, I need to sit down to collect myself.

It wasn't really the bus that's making me ill. It's that I'm about to do something completely out of character. Obsessively anal, highly neurotic, overscheduled teenaged girls don't lie to their new boyfriends (and father—I told him I was out with Cherise) then take a bus across town to go to a bar, the invitation for which was mysteriously handed to her by some strange boy.

I put my head between my knees and take a few deep breaths. The realization hits that I have no idea what or who I'm going to find at the Holy Grail. Part of me, the biggest part, wants to sit here until the next bus comes and catch a ride back home. This was a stupid idea. I could be walking into danger. Maybe some psychotic stalker gave me that invitation and the gory details of my demise will lead tomorrow's news headlines.

Then again, I've come this far. I might as well see it through.

I decide to give my imagination a rest and, getting up from the bench, point my feet toward the Holy Grail. What good are cute boots and a stylin' jacket if you don't take them out every once in a while? I'm going in!

At the door, the bouncers are handing wristbands to anyone over twenty-one. Without a wristband, I order a Sprite, then make my way to the front of the room, near the dance floor. A band is playing. They're actually pretty good. A lot of people are dancing.

The Holy Grail is packed. Most of the people inside are college-aged, probably from the University of Cincinnati or maybe Miami of Ohio. I don't see anyone I know and again, I wonder what has possessed me to come here.

A guy named Bill, or Phil, (it's really loud in here) asks me to dance. I turn him down. I'm positive I didn't come here to dance with a guy wearing a plaid sweater vest.

The band finishes their set and a DJ takes over while the next band sets up. I've been here a half hour so far, and I still have no idea what I'm doing here. I'll give my mysterious invitation sender another twenty minutes to make the big reveal, then I'm going home. The club seems like a fun place, the energy is electric, but I'm alone. Being at a bar alone is very similar to eating alone. I don't like either one. You can only watch other people have fun for so long before you have to either quit or join in. In twenty minutes, I'm planning to quit.

The DJ spins another song, then the bar goes dark. A spinning strobe announces that a new band is about to begin. This is obviously the band that people have come tonight to see. There is a crush as people rush to the base of the stage. The dance floor no longer has any room for dancing, and I am pressed up to the base of the stage between Bill/Phil and a college girl wearing a bra as if it were a shirt.

There's so much screaming and cheering that I miss the announced introduction of the band. I turn to bra girl to ask what the announcer said, but she's now making out with Bill/Phil. I wonder if they know each other. I bet not. I'm pretty sure they met over my head and behind my back, since until a few minutes ago, I was standing between them. I briefly wonder if bra girl is feeling fireworks from the kiss.

The drummer has begun the set. Sitting alone under a spotlight, he's wearing black. Black T-shirt, black jeans, black boots. He's banging out a rhythm and the crowd is stirring wildly, hands pumping in the air to the beat.

A bass guitarist joins the drummer. Then another guitarist, acoustic this time. I'm starting to feel those butterflies again in my stomach. With blinding clarity, I know for sure they aren't caused by the bus fumes. This time, they're in anticipation.

I now know who it was that braved Gavin Masterson's house party and gave twenty bucks to some kid to deliver an invitation to me. I should have guessed.

There's an excitement in the crowd as the band begins to play together. Only one last musical position needs to be filled. I'm shoved up against the stage base with a perfect view of that still-empty seat. It sits in front of the keyboards.

A little drum solo. A guitar jam. A bass rhythm. And then, the spotlight focuses on the guy walking across the stage. Black cargo pants. Black T-shirt. Black tennis shoes. And a shiny silver earring.

Tyler Gregory winks at me and then begins to play.

Nineteen

There is something going on that
you do not fully understand.
www.astrology4stars.com

"Sylvie!" I hear my name called from somewhere behind me. I know that voice as well
as my own. It's Cherise.

She and Nathan shove their way
through the crowd toward me. I hear her
saying, "Excuse me," over and over again as
they barrel forward.

Cherise wedges herself between me and
Bill/Phil. She and Nathan are holding hands
and I immediately notice that she's holding
as tightly to him as he is to her. They look
like they are actually enjoying the whole

handholding thing, sweaty palms and all.

"I thought you'd be out with Adam tonight," Cherise says. "What are you doing here?" She's screaming, three millimeters from my ear and still, I can barely hear her.

What am I doing here? That's a loaded question. There is the short answer: Tyler invited me. And the long answer, which begins the day I lost the diamond out of my mother's ring and ends here at the Holy Grail watching Silent Knight in concert.

The long answer is too confusing. The truth is, I have no idea what I'm doing here. I'll shoot for the short answer and see what happens.

"Tyler invited me," I say simply.

"He did?" Cherise asks. I nod, then in an attempt to get out of any further conversation, I turn to Nathan and say, "Hey."

With his free hand, Nathan gives me a little hug. I smile. He's a nice guy and he and Cherise seem good together.

In the pause between songs, Cherise tells me that this is Silent Knight's first big gig. They hired a manager, who's doing great things for the band. Once Tyler graduates and the guys can devote themselves full-time to their music, Cherise thinks that they might really have a chance at hitting the music scene huge.

Those butterflies I was feeling have converted to a groundswell of warmth. I'm filled with pride. My best friend's brother. *My* friend Tyler Gregory rocks the house.

Silent Knight takes three encores. They play until they run out of their own original music and have to start playing radio covers.

After the concert, Tyler is swarmed by fans. We can't get near him, so we hang off to the side waiting for the crowd to thin. Most of his admirers are girls, who are thrusting small slips of paper at him with their phone numbers written in lipstick. He pockets the numbers, but I see him look over at me a few times, and it almost seems like he's gauging my reaction. What do I care if college girls are coming on to him? I have a boyfriend. A boyfriend who's taking me to prom next weekend.

Cherise grows quickly bored with waiting for her brother and tells him to catch up with us at the Corner Café. By the time we leave the club, it's late. I've called my father to extend my curfew. He said that as long as I was in the neighborhood, which includes the café, I could have an extra hour.

I feel better now that I'm not lying to my father anymore. One lie is more than I can emotionally handle at a time. Now I really am out with Cherise. And Nathan. And once he breaks free from his adoring public, Tyler will be joining us, too.

No bus for me. Nathan has wheels. And as fate would have it, Nathan's car is a hybrid. I run my fingers through my hair and wonder why Cherise and Nathan never got together before now. They are kindred souls.

Dotty shows us to a booth by the window and hands us each a menu. It's past midnight now and the place is pretty much deserted. Clearly Cherise has been bringing Nathan here pretty often, as she asks us what we were up to tonight and Cherise tells her about Tyler's big concert.

"That boy's gonna be famous some day," Dotty tells us. "Mark my words."

Cherise agrees. "The band was great tonight."

"How's Jonathan Miller's family doing?" Dotty asks Cherise. "I think about him nearly everyday."

"Me, too," Cherise says. A second ago, I though I was part of the conversation, or at least knew what was going on; now suddenly

I'm out. I have no idea who Jonathan Miller is. And, by the look on his face, neither does Nathan.

Dotty pinches her lips together and says, "Tell Alex 'hey' for me, when you see him next."

"Will do," Cherise says, then we all order.

When Dotty retreats to the kitchen, I turn to Cherise. "Who's Jonathan Miller? Or Alex?"

"You remember Jonathan, don't you?" Cherise toys with the edge of her paper napkin, tearing off a sliver and rolling it between her fingers into a ball.

I'm about to swear I've never heard of him, but then I put it all together. Just to be sure, I ask, "Is Jonathan the same as J.J.?"

A shadow passes Cherise's eyes and for a minute, I think maybe she's going to tear up.

Nathan gives me a questioning look and I explain, "J.J. Miller was one of the original members of Silent Knight." I know the story, even though I never actually met J.J. "He was the drummer. Jonathan was two years older than us."

Cherise jumps in, reminding me that the band's members were from Tyler's junior high school soccer league. Jonathan was one of the oldest players on the team, Tyler, one of the youngest. She leans her head onto Nathan's shoulder for support as she continues the story.

"Right out of high school, J.J. joined the army." Cherise gets that moist-foggy look in her eyes again. "His unit was taken directly from basic training and dropped in the middle of Baghdad."

"Go on," Nathan gently prods.

"He was killed by a roadside bomb less than a month after he deployed." Cherise says all that on one breath, as if the words themselves are so painful that they need to be said quickly and gotten over with as fast as possible.

It comes back to me in a flood of memory. At the time, I was visiting my mother's cousin in Kentucky. It was the one week I've ever taken off from work. By the time I got back, J.J.'s death was old news, the funeral was over, and Cherise didn't want to talk about it.

"Those Miller boys used to come in here all the time with their dad," Dotty chimes in as she returns to our table carrying our drinks. "The parents were divorced. Mr. Miller would have the boys two weekends a month. They'd drop by for Sunday brunch. It was a tradition." Dotty sets the waters on the table and puts her hands on her hips. "After Jonathan died, Mr. Miller stopped coming in. Now and again he'll pop by, but I think there are too many memories in this place for him to handle."

"Who's Alex?" I ask after a respectable silent pause. For me, the story began and ended with Jonathan's death.

"J.J.'s kid brother," Cherise answers as Dotty goes to welcome new customers. "He took over the drummer position for the band."

There's a question niggling at the back of my mind. It's been there since Tyler told me to "ask Cherise," a couple weeks ago. I never did and now, it feels somehow connected.

"Why does Tyler wear only black?" I ask slowly, as if the question is as big and important as "What is the meaning of life?" In my head I can distinctly see the other members of Silent Knight dressed the same as Tyler.

"When Jonathan shipped out," Cherise says tossing her little napkin ball and ripping off another strip from the tissue, "the band agreed that they would only wear black until Jonathan came home safely." Cherise snuggles in tighter to Nathan. "None of them is willing to break the pact.

Even after the funeral, the guys have kept on wearing black."

Has it really only been two years that Tyler has been dressing in black? Funny how the memory can play tricks on a person. I'd swear it was forever. But now that I'm thinking about it, maybe it has only been the last few years. I am bringing up a picture of Tyler, sitting on his living room rug, reading a book, wearing khaki pants and a striped T-shirt. It must have been the beginning of our sophomore year because I'm certain that Cherise and I were on the couch reviewing notes for our first algebra exam of the semester.

Cherise pulls herself away from Nathan and leans forward. "Do you know how hard it is to find organic fabric dyes in black? The stuff has no holding power. One wash and his shirts fade to gray." She smiles and the tension is broken.

"Does he have any plans to add color in the near future?" I ask.

"No," Tyler answers. The conversation was so intense that nobody noticed he had arrived. I wonder how long he'd been standing by the booth, listening. He sits down next to me, saying, "I might go on dressed like Zorro for the remainder of my days."

He tells me that when the guys made the pact, they'd tacked on wearing the requisite black cloaks as a joke. They never expected that J.J. wasn't coming home.

"J.J. would love knowing that he single-handedly ruined the individual fashions of his three best friends and brother, too." Tyler shrugs. "I regret that pact every day since we made it. What I'd give to wear white underwear!"

I nearly laugh. I had wondered about Tyler's underwear once before.

The conversation moves from Jonathan Miller and the war in Iraq to the band's big news. Apparently their new manager got them another gig next Saturday night. Tyler will find out the details in a few days.

Cherise and Nathan immediately remind Tyler that next Saturday is prom night. He knew that, but since he's not going, it doesn't matter. "You're a great sis," he tells Cherise, "but you don't have to be at every gig."

"While you're playing the clubs, I'll come when I can, but mostly be with you in spirit," she says. "But when you hit it big, you'd better save me a seat at the Grammys," Cherise adds with a laugh. She glances at Nathan, then amends, "Two seats."

I want to go to the Grammys, too. But it seems silly to throw that out there. I mean, not that Tyler might not make it to the Grammy Awards, but because Tyler and I don't really have a relationship. It would be too weird for him to include me on his VIP list.

The café is closing. It's time for us all to go home.

Cherise walks Nathan to his car. Tyler and I start walking toward our apartment building together. That usually comfortable silence between us feels heavy. There are things that need to be said, but how to begin?

"Thanks for inviting me tonight," I say, letting Tyler know that I figured out he was the one who hired the mysterious delivery guy at Gavin Masterson's party.

"You're welcome," Tyler says simply. With that, the conversation about the invitation is opened and closed.

Speaking of Gavin Masterson, Tyler and I are about three blocks from our apartment building when we run into him. Not literally, but pretty darn close. He pops out of a bar almost at the exact same time as we pass the doorway. And to my great surprise, Adam's with him.

"Hi," I say sheepishly, looking from

Adam to the sign above the GLOBETROTTER BAR. I'm experiencing that horribly uncomfortable flushed feeling that you get when you've been caught in a lie. Wait a second! What's Adam doing at a bar? And why's he alone with Gavin?

"I thought you were going to the movies tonight?" I ask, after Adam has returned my "Hi" with an awkward one of his own.

"I did," he tells me. He'd told me he was going with some guys from the swim team. Unfortunately, I didn't ask who. "Afterward, Gavin and I went out for a drink."

Gavin, who is leaning very heavily on Adam, bends toward me. He reeks of beer and his eyes can't seem to focus on me. "I made us fake IDs," he brags. "Worked like a charm." His eyes finally meet mine, though just for an instant while he adds, "I'll make you one too, if you want, Sylvie."

"No thanks," I tell him, stepping back out of the path of his breath.

Shifting his feet to gain better balance, Adam straightens Gavin up, glances at Tyler, then asks me, "I thought you were staying home tonight."

"I—" I don't know what to say. Even coming out of a bar, where he's been drinking on a fake ID, Adam is still more honorable than I will ever be. At least he went to the movie first, just like he said he was going to. I—well—I knew I was going out when I told him I wasn't. I completely lied to him.

"I—" I begin again only to be cut short by Gavin who has peeled himself off Adam and is now wobbling toward me.

"Sharing!" Gavin slurs as he grabs onto my shoulders for support. "Swim team is all about sharing, right Adam?"

"Sure, Gavin," Adam agrees as he tries to pull Gavin off me. "Whatever you say," Adam is placating Gavin while coaxing him to let me go.

"We share towels, goggles, and now," Gavin grabs me more fully, hanging on with his arms practically circling my neck, "let's share Sylvie." It happens so fast, I don't have time to duck. Gavin slams his lips against mine.

I'm not scared. Really. I'm just grossed out.

I don't for one second think Gavin is going to rape me right here on the street or anything like that. I believe with all my heart that Gavin's a bully, not a criminal. With one gross kiss, he's letting Adam know that no matter how good a swimmer Adam might be or how popular Adam is around school, Gavin's still the boss. And I'm an unfortunate pawn in his superiority game.

Disgust propels my struggle to break free, but Gavin's an athlete and I'm a science geek, and a girl. He easily overpowers me. Then again, he's drunk and I'm not, so I bring up my knee, slamming it into his crotch as hard as I can.

"Oof." Gavin instinctively bends over to protect himself from further assault and in doing so, stumbles. Trying to regain his footing, he grabs me harder and the two of us tumble to the ground.

I hear Tyler shout. And Adam, too, but I can't make out what they are saying.

The whole thing lasts no more than a few seconds, but a few seconds with Gavin slobbering on top of me seems like a lifetime. If we're rating kisses, his don't even approach human. I'm completely repulsed.

Next thing I know, Adam's pulled Gavin away. And Tyler's helping me up.

"Are you okay?" Tyler asks as I spit onto the sidewalk and then wipe my mouth with the back of my hand.

I tell him I'm fine. "Do all drunk guys

slobber like that? Or is it just Gavin?" I ask, trying to lighten the moment and assure Tyler that I'm okay at the same time.

He gives a small laugh, saying, "I can't say as I've ever kissed a drunk guy before, so I really wouldn't know." And with a grin, he adds, "And I'm not planning to plant a big, juicy one on Gavin anytime soon."

Tyler puts his arm around me protectively and gives me a reassuring squeeze.

"I'm so sorry, Sylvie," Adam tells me as he props Gavin back up, leaning him heavily against his side. "Gavin talks about 'sharing' at all the swim team meetings; I had no idea *you* were part of what he meant."

From the night at Gavin's party, I knew exactly what Gavin had in mind. I just never expected Gavin to jump me on the street, or anywhere else for that matter. But I don't tell Adam that. I simply accept his apology with a nod.

"He's so drunk, he won't remember this tomorrow." Adam is clearly taken aback by his friend's behavior. "I'm Gavin's designated driver tonight. Even if he is acting like a jerk, I promised I'd make sure he got home safely." Always the gentleman, that's my Adam.

"I'll call you in a little while." Adam has

an indescribable expression on his face. "I'm sorry, Sylvie," he repeats. And with that, Adam starts to head off, dragging Gavin away from us.

"Hey Adam, you're not the one who needs to apologize," Tyler calls to Adam's back.

Adam turns, repositioning Gavin, who's teetering on the edge of consciousness.

"What?" Adam stares at Tyler with a surprised look on his face. "What'd you say?"

"You don't have anything to apologize for," Tyler says firmly, pointing at Gavin. "But Gavin does."

Recognizing his own name, Gavin straightens up on his own legs. Adam isn't letting him go, but Gavin has returned to the land of the lucid. At least for a moment.

Gavin spurts out, "I'm not apologi—" But then, something stops him midspeech. He looks up and for the first time seems to notice Tyler's presence.

Cherise tells me later it apparently wasn't a phone call from Cherise's father that stopped Gavin's harassment in fourth grade. It was a "meeting" between Gavin and Tyler in the boy's bathroom after school that did it. I didn't notice that Gavin took a few "sick" days before the end of the term that year. I do, however, vaguely recall Tyler having a long scratch under his eye, but I'm pretty sure Cherise told me it was from flipping off his skateboard (Tyler was a skatehead in elementary school).

Whatever transpired between Tyler and Gavin that day, I'll never know for sure. But by the time spring term began, Gavin had found new prey. He never bothered Cherise again.

And, I have to say, judging by the look that Tyler is currently giving Gavin, Gavin won't be bugging me again either.

"Sorry, Sylvie," Gavin mutters, diverting his eyes, staring down at his feet.

Tyler clears his throat.

Gavin raises his drunk eyes up to my sober ones and repeats, "Sorry."

At that, Tyler smiles and says to Adam, "*Now*, you can take him home."

Adam simply agrees, then says to me, "I'll call you in a few."

"Okay," I reply. I'll be glad for the conversation. Even with all that's happened tonight, I still feel the need to explain why I wasn't at home, like I said I would be. I suppose I'll tell Adam the basic truth: I was invited to hear Tyler's band play.

Tyler and I walk the rest of the way home together, in silence.

Imagine my surprise to find Madame Jakarta sitting on the front steps. She's wearing a full black skirt, a lavender wrap sweater and, would you believe it, panty hose. Her long dark hair is pulled back in a barrette. It's a bit like when I saw her that one time in the grocery store, wearing jeans. I feel thrown off by her appearance. I think I'm more comfortable when my psychic advisor wears a muumuu and turban.

Madame Jakarta stands as Tyler and I approach. She greets us each by name, then turns to me. She isn't looking at Tyler at all. All her energy is focused in my direction.

"I see you've finally begun your quest," Madame Jakarta says with a smile. Then, with a toss of her head and a swish of her skirt, she disappears around the building and vanishes into the shadows.

"Quest? What quest?" I call after her retreating figure. Then I remember that she mentioned a quest the day she did my palm reading.

I suppose I really have been paying attention all along.

Twenty

It's been an odd few days.

Tyler has been strangely absent since Saturday night. I try to tell myself that I don't care where he is or what he's up to, but after two days of going to lunch and the Corner Café without him shadowing Cherise, my curiosity takes over and I finally ask Cherise where he's been.

"He's rehearsing," Cherise tells me. "Every free second he gets, he's working on the music for the band's Saturday-night gig." That explains it. Mostly. What's really weird is that I haven't seen him in the hall at school. It seems like he might be avoiding me. Nah. I'm just overthinking things once again. It's like Cherise says, he's busy with the band.

Adam, on the other hand, has been overwhelmingly present. That night on the phone, Adam told me that he wouldn't be hanging out with Gavin anymore. I said that I honestly didn't care if he did. After seeing the expression on Gavin's face when Tyler made him apologize to me, there's no way Gavin will try "sharing" with Adam ever again.

At lunch period, Adam continues to pop over to the swim table, but now he doesn't linger there. And though Gavin still scoots over to make room for him, Adam always sits at the other end of the table.

All things considered, Wednesday's shaping up to be a really great day. I got an A on an English Lit paper. Another A on a pop quiz in psych. After school, Laila Halaby, head cook at the Corner Café, was trying a new raspberry pie recipe, so Cherise and I got a free taste test. What could be better than that?

Only one thing . . . and it's waiting for

me in my mailbox when I get home from work: A pale white envelope with the Yale crest embossed in the upper-left-hand corner.

I see the familiar Hebrew lettering, drawn on the pages of an open book. I've looked at this crest a thousand times. Researched its meaning. If you're going to Yale, you gotta know what the historic crest says. The Hebrew says, "In Light and Truth." Around it is the Latin, *Lux et Veritas*, meaning the same thing. There couldn't be anything be better than going to a school whose motto is "In Light and Truth." Could there?

I hold that envelope as if it contains the most delicate jewel, gingerly carrying it into the apartment and setting it on the kitchen table. I stare at the Yale crest for a full minute, heart racing, before finally mustering the courage to slip my finger under one corner of the sealed flap.

I try my best to be slow and deliberate about ripping the envelope. But I can't. My heart's pounding in my head and there are goose bumps popping out all over my arms. When I can't take it anymore, I tear at the envelope like a lion eating a gazelle. Chunks of the envelope fall to the floor. It's then that I slow down. I lift the letter toward the light, peeking through the vellum to see if I can read the word "accepted" or "rejected."

The paper's too thick to read through. I'm going to have to unfold the letter.

So, very cautiously, with shaking hands, I do.

Application accepted.

My future has arrived.

I got the scholarship! I got it! Wahoo!

I immediately call my father at the tux shop. He was finishing up the day's accounting when I cut out to go home. He answers the shop line and we have a quick, "I got it!" "Congratulations," conversation. He'll be home in an hour and we'll have dinner then. Unlike other parents who might suggest going out to celebrate, he tells me there's chicken that needs defrosting. I hang up, certain that he's proud, but also wishing he could say it out loud. Just this once.

Dinner's a quiet affair, like always. After I spoke to my father, I called Cherise with the news. We were finishing up dinner when she came by with a gift. Garnet earrings. I thought it was an odd present until she explained that garnet was the state mineral of Connecticut. And since Yale is in Connecticut . . . she thought it was appropriate. I tell her that the earrings are a wonderful gift and immediately put them on.

A little homework after dinner, then I start to sew. Adam said he'd stop by after a mandatory swim team meeting. It seems that there's a heated discussion about switching the swimsuit colors to red and blue instead of blue and red. It's become a huge deal and there's a meeting tonight to vote on the matter.

I sit at the sewing machine putting the finishing touches on Tanisha's gown.

I completed Jennifer's nymph outfit last night and gave it to her at school this morning. I'll give Tanisha hers first thing tomorrow. There's still a lot to do on my Cinderella costume, but after tonight, I'll have two nights and most of Saturday to get it done. I might be able to squeeze in a bit of sewing if things are uncharacteristically quiet at the tuxedo shop Saturday morning. I can't believe that prom is only three days away! Where did the time go?

I think back to those few days when I tried to adhere to a tight schedule and smile to myself. Life can certainly get in the way of even the best-formulated plans. Over the past month, my life has taken turns I never could have imagined. And yet, I'm still the same old Sylvie. Organized, neurotic, controlling, and completely focused on academics. Yep, that's me.

I add some golden lace to the bottom of Tanisha's dress, then reconsidering, remove the lace and tack it to the sleeves instead. I have some seed pearls left over from that wedding dress we have displayed in the tux shop window. I move Tanisha's dress to the sewing table and glue the beads randomly along the bottom of the velvet dress where the lace was meant to be. I hope that Tanisha doesn't mind the change, but she didn't mind the first time, when I added the slit to her underdress.

Speaking of the underdress, it needs to be hemmed. Hemming is what I do best.

I am so deeply engrossed in sewing that I don't hear the doorbell when it rings. Before I know it, Adam is in my room, standing behind me. He doesn't kiss me, but he's close enough that I feel his breath on the back of my neck. "Your dad let me in," he tells me. "Get your stuff. We don't want to be late."

"Late? For what?"

He steps back from me, giving me room to get up from my chair and face him.

"Astronomy club," Adam replies. "Hurry up."

"Huh?" My jaw is hanging slack. "What are you talking about?"

Adam looks at me like I have missed something huge. "Didn't you get the e-mail?"

I stare at him blankly. I have no idea what he's talking about.

"Mrs. Kelsow called an astronomy club meeting tonight," Adam explains. "There's going to be a partial lunar eclipse. She didn't mention it at the last club meeting because it was supposed to be too cloudy to see, but the winds picked up and pushed the clouds away. Viewing should be awesome." He asks me where my telescope bag is and then says, "We better hurry. We don't want to miss it."

A partial lunar eclipse! Part of the moon is about to pass through the Earth's umbral shadow. I should have known an eclipse was coming. I usually keep track of these things. Where's my head lately? I can't believe I nearly missed seeing an eclipse. I've been so busy sewing that I failed to check my e-mail! You have to love that Adam is watching out for me.

Adam slips my telescope bag over his shoulder and says, "Let's get out of here."

I need shoes. My Keds are under the sewing table. I reach down to pick them up and tip over the bottle of glue. It's then I realize that I only put seed pearls on the front part of Tanisha's gown. In order to go out tonight, I'd have to put off finishing her dress for a day. And if I do that, I'll never have enough time to complete my own costume before the prom.

But a partial lunar eclipse! They only happen a couple of times a year.

I snatch up my shoes and sit down at my desk to put them on. One shoe on. One off, when the realization hits me like an anvil to the head. I drop my shoe. It clunks to the floor.

"I can't go." I tell Adam about Tanisha's dress and how I've got to finish it tonight. Being Adam, he offers to help. He's willing to skip the eclipse to glue beads onto the dress with me.

I can see he's just trying to be nice. It's obvious he'd rather go to astronomy club. With or without me.

"Go on," I tell him. "You should take

advantage of the opportunity. I'll come next time," I say, though something inside me is wondering where each of us will be the next time an eclipse happens.

Adam sets down my telescope. "We'll catch up tomorrow," he says as he leaves the apartment.

I take up a handful of seed pearls and begin laying them out on the dress material. I'm precise in their positioning. The vision of where they should go is as clear as the night sky over Cincinnati.

A sense of pride washes over me as I begin to glue down them down. There are hours of work stretching before me, but in the back of my mind, I can see the finished costume. It'll be beautiful. This is a completely different kind of pride than when I got the news of the Yale scholarship. . . .

The scholarship! I can't believe I haven't told Adam that I got it. He's been such an integral part of my focused determination over the past month. He's quizzed me and coached me and helped me keep my grades up. Adam has shown me that it is possible to have a boyfriend and pursue my dreams at the same time.

And here I didn't think to phone him

after I opened the letter, and the scholarship never crossed my mind while he was in my room.

I think about why as I place two more beads on Tanisha's dress. The reason comes to me in a blinding flash and I shove the lid down on the glue. I'll finish Tanisha's costume tomorrow night. Tonight, I'm going to see the eclipse.

I snatch up my telescope bag and head out. Adam's at the park. It would be the perfect time to tell him about Yale. But I'm not going to the park.

I'm going up instead. Up to the roof.

I'm hoping I won't be alone.

Twenty-one

Ditch your inhibitions. It's time for a change.
www.astrology4stars.com

I open the door and step outside. I sniff the air, hoping to smell wood and earth, but no, the roof is dark and deserted.

Examining the sky with my naked eye, I search for signs of the eclipse, then stop myself. Tonight, I'm not going to be an astronomer. This is not an academic encounter with outer space. No, this is me standing on that middle ground between astrology and astronomy. I'm looking up in awe to witness the sun and the moon intersect. No thoughts about why or how it happens. I'm enjoying the view. That's all. That's enough.

As the sun peeks out from behind the moon, I think about my mom. With the passing years, her memory has faded. I know I look like her, but I wish I could recall the way she walked or how she laughed; did she snort? Or cover her mouth when she giggled? Was it from her chest or a rumble from her stomach? I struggle to remember the cadence of her voice. I wish I could remember all the little details better. I wish she could hold me close. I wish she was here.

"Mom?" I say softly, my words rising on the whisper of wind. "I need you."

"We both do." My father's voice rides on a breeze blowing behind my back. I turn to look at him. He's coming through the rooftop door. "We both do," he says again, then comes toward me, arms outstretched. "There was something about the way you looked tonight when you left the apartment, I thought you might like some company."

It wasn't my dad who I hoped would be on the roof tonight, but he's right. I do want company and he's offering.

I can't speak, because I start to cry. Without a word, my father pulls me into a bear hug, so warm and comfortable and tight that I cry even harder.

"I've missed so many opportunities," he says. "Now you're headed off to college and I wish I could get those moments back."

Without breaking his hold, he slips his hand into his suit pocket and hands me a handkerchief. I take it and blow my nose. I've never known what to do with a borrowed handkerchief after you've blown your nose into it. But my father does. He takes it from me, snot and all, and slips it back into his pocket. Only when my tears have stopped does he pull away to take a long look at me.

My father brushes a finger over my cheek, carrying off the last remaining tear.

"I love you, Sylvie," he says. "I haven't done a very good job of showing you over the years, but I do, you know."

I nod because if I say anything I'll start to cry again. The truth is, I've always known he loves me. In his own quiet way, Dad's always been there. Even when he was simply sitting on my bed, or silently reading his paper at breakfast. Sometimes, he even started a conversation with me, asking how or why, on those occasions it was me who kept us at a distance. I chose not to engage.

Tonight, he's opened the door. Head held high, I am going to walk through it.

"Dad?" I begin the conversation I came to talk to Mom about. "Have you ever wondered why I want to go to Yale to study astronomy?"

"You've always wanted to walk in your mom's footsteps," my father says, seemingly puzzled. "Have you changed your mind?

"Not really." Then, I admit, "Well, sort of."

"Are you all right?" He looks worried. My father doesn't ask for the details of what's happened. He just leaves his question, his concern for me, hanging in the cool night air. He might not be a man of many words, but in this moment, he's asked the right ones.

"I'll be okay," I tell him. "I'm not sure what I want, yet," I pause to change conversational direction. "How'd you know Mom was the one for you?"

My father takes a step back from me and turns. He heads over to the edge of the rooftop and peers out at the night sky. I follow.

"There was magic in her kisses," he tells me, and instinctively I know if I could turn up the brilliance of the stars, I'd see tears in his eyes. There are tears in mine. I don't ask for the handkerchief again, choosing to wipe my face on my sleeve instead.

"Yeah," I say. "I figured you'd say that." We look out at the stars for a while, side by side. Daughter and Dad.

My father finally breaks the silence. "Well?" he says. Even though we're in the midst of our big reconciliation, should I have expected him to speak in a complete sentence? He's still the guy he was a half hour ago. It's me who's changed.

"Well, what?" I ask him.

"Ask her," he says simply.

"Ask who what?"

"You came up here tonight to ask your mother a question."

"No I didn't," I begin to protest. "I came to see the eclipse."

"Are you sure?" I know he's encouraging me to say whatever's on my mind.

"I suppose—Oh," I reply, surprising myself when a question comes to me like a supernova explosion. I suddenly know exactly what I want. There are two things and one of them I can have right now. All I have to do is ask.

"Mom," I call out into the night. "Would you be terribly disappointed if I didn't go to Yale?"

"Tell her why," my father prods. "She'll want to know the reason." It feels as if he knew I was coming to this decision all along. Maybe he did. He might not have commented, but he's been around a lot lately. Watching. Wondering. And waiting for me to acknowledge what's been inside me all along: I'm my father's daughter. As much, or perhaps even more, than my mother's.

"Mom," I say boldly, looking up at the stars and watching them blink at me. Or are they winking? "I still want to be an astronomer," I tell her. "But I also want to sew. If I go to Case Western Reserve, I can study astronomy and keep making costumes with Jennifer and Tanisha." I pause, wondering if I need to explain who Jennifer and Tanisha are, then decide she already knows. "They offered to pay me to sew for them once, maybe I can do it to earn money while I'm at school," I tell her. Then turning away from the stars, I look at my father and add, "Astronomy's in my heart. Sewing's in my blood."

He smiles at me and wraps his arm around me. "She's proud of you no matter what you do," he tells me. Then adds in a whisper near my ear, "I am, too."

"What about the Yale scholarship?" Being practical, I'm going to need to work out the details of my college shift.

"I bet Case Western has scholarships, too." He grins and adds, "I'm glad you'll be in state. Yale was too far away."

I smile warmly at my dad and then, together, we turn to look up at the sky.

The eclipse is beautiful. But it's a shooting star that seals my fate.

As a future astronomer, I can tell you, on the average night shooting stars occur every ten to fifteen minutes. But as Sylvie Townsend, daughter of Bernard and Miriam Townsend, I know this particular star was shooting just for me.

Twenty-two

Follow your instincts. Trust your gut.
www.astrology4stars.com

I ask Adam to meet me at the Corner Café after swimming practice is over. This isn't a date. Not a real one, at least. What's the opposite of "date"? Undate? Antidate?

No matter what you call it, it's time.

Time to tell him what I've been thinking.

Time to break up.

Breakups suck. Even when you know for certain that you're doing the right thing, they suck. This is my first breakup so it has an added layer of extra sucky-ness.

Adam sits across from me in the booth. I take a sip of water, as much to steel my nerves as to keep my hands out of his reach. I don't want to be holding hands with him when I tell him.

"Adam," I begin, then stop. I rehearsed this last night. It went smoothly in front of my bathroom mirror. My heart wasn't racing the Indianapolis 500 and sweat wasn't dripping down my back. I close my eyes and begin again.

"This relationship isn't working for me," I say in one breath. "I want to break up." Okay, so that wasn't very eloquent, but in a pressured moment, I couldn't have done any better.

Adam sits silently soaking in the full impact of what I've said then asks simply, "Why?" He doesn't look torn up or like he's going to cry or anything like that, he just looks surprised. As if he expected a different conversation entirely when he came to meet me.

"Something isn't clicking for me." I don't know exactly how to explain, so I stumble on my words as I say, "It's not you. You're amazing. Awesome. You're definitely a prince charming, or a superman, just not mine."

Adam doesn't look like he is ready to formulate a response, so I ramble on.

"It's like a puzzle," I tell him, using the only metaphor that makes sense. "You're so stoked when you get to the last few pieces. You've spent hours working on it. It's been fun and great. But then, you discover a few pieces don't fit. No matter how hard you try to force them, they're the wrong shape or color."

Like when your boyfriend thinks your dream is a cute hobby, or if he's part of a social group that makes you uncomfortable no matter how hard you try, or the kisses just aren't right. Then there's also the problem that you can't stop thinking about someone else.

"If the last pieces don't slip into place, the whole puzzle's off and you have to stop trying to force it."

Adam nods. "Is this about what happened with Gavin?" he asks. "You know I don't hang out with him anymore."

"I know," I assure him. "This has nothing to do with Gavin." Not directly, anyway. "A lot of the puzzle pieces are out of whack."

He sighs. "I suppose we were going to have to break up eventually."

"Huh?" Graceful, eh? I sound like a

screech owl, but come on, how could he possibly have known what I was thinking?

"Oh, Sylvie," he says, reaching out and peeling my hands off my water glass, where they've been this whole time. He takes my hands in his. "I like you. I really like you. But I'm not in love with you." He squeezes my hands. "You're fun to be with. Smart. Clever. And a good kisser."

Did I just hear him correctly? He thinks I'm a good kisser!

"But I'm not looking to fall in love," he tells me. "Like you and Yale, I have college dreams, too." I suddenly feel bad that I never told him I got the scholarship. Or that I've turned it down.

Adam releases my hands. "I wanted to go to prom with you. After that there's only a month before graduation; we'd have had to go our separate ways at that point anyway. I was going to talk to you after the dance." He smiles. "You have your dreams and I have mine. Our path together would eventually come to an end."

He gives me a sweet look and adds, "Unless you've decided to go to UCLA."

I smile. "No, thanks." There's no reason to tell him I faxed over a new scholarship application to Case Western this morning.

"I didn't think so." Maybe he knows me a little better than I'm giving him credit for.

My heartbeat has settled back to normal. The sweat on my back has dried.

"It wasn't meant to be," I say.

"Nope," Adam agrees. Then he offers, "We can still go to the prom together if you want." He quickly adds, "As friends."

I think about it for a second. I chose viewing the eclipse (and hanging out with my dad), over making the Cinderella dress. I'd have to work myself to the bone if I want to wear it tomorrow night and that seems . . . well . . . pointless.

"I don't think so," I tell him. But then I grow concerned. I don't want Adam to have to go alone, and he did rent a costume for the dance.

"Would you mind if I asked Melanie?" he asks me. "We hung out last night during the eclipse and I think she'd like to go."

I start to ask who Melanie is, but quickly realize she's Mrs. Kelsow's daughter. I smile. "Sounds good."

It's getting late. We decide to go ahead and have dinner together. One final hurrah for our romance and a first step for our friendship.

And as I order the spaghetti, I can't help but feel deeply satisfied.

I'm beginning to think that nearly four weeks after the diamond fell out of my mother's ring, it's possible that I've changed. I'm not same old neurotic Sylvie anymore.

I've discovered that days are more fun without a schedule. People are much more interesting when they're cloaked in mystery. And I have to admit, I now believe that maybe there is something real about Cherise's predictions. They all came true. Well, kind of. She said that I'd meet a guy on Wednesday, he'd ask me to prom, and that I'd fall in love. I met a guy that Wednesday and he asked me to prom (though it took two tries to get the invitation).

Falling in love was only one thing she totally botched. Cherise said that when "Neptune's moon was high in the sky, a guy who loves you and whom you love will ask you to dance." I got asked to prom, but not by a guy I love. He doesn't love me either.

If you include the freak blizzard and all the times she's intuited our exam questions,

I'm finally willing to consider astrology might not be as ridiculous as I thought. Even a professional statistician would have to say she's well within the margin of error.

She was close, real close, but in the end, Adam and I weren't written in the stars after all.

A wise man once said that the stars provide opportunity. It's up to me to make my own destiny. He told me that the stars can both illuminate the sky and give courage to the soul. I believe now that my destiny waits in that middle place where astronomy and astrology intertwine.

As of this very minute, I've begun to sculpt my own destiny.

Phase one is now complete.

Phase two is just beginning.

Twenty-three

You are older and wiser than
you were yesterday.
www.astrology4stars.com

"I'm *not* going to the Spring Fling dance tonight." That's what I tell Jennifer and Tanisha the fifteenth time they call. They called a bunch of times while I was at home, then after I turned off my cell phone, they managed to track me down at the tuxedo shop.

One calls. Then the other. Back and forth like it's a tennis match.

"*Pleeease,*" Jennifer begs me. "We can still go together like we planned. You can dance with Jordan if you want." The thought of me dancing with a big tree flashes through my brain. It's hard not to laugh.

"I'm not going," I tell Jennifer. "I never finished the Cinderella dress."

"Wear my nymph costume," Jennifer says. "I'll wear a paper bag if you'll say you'll come with us." Jennifer wouldn't offer me her costume if she didn't mean it. All those years I passed judgment on her and I was wrong. Jennifer's a nice person. A good friend. Tanisha, too.

They were thrilled when they heard that I was going to shoot for a scholarship to Case Western instead of going to Yale. They even offered to change the name of their design-team to JT&S Costumes. I turned them down. I'm still planning to major in astronomy. I might, however, be the first astronomer ever to minor in costume design. We'll see. For now, I want to be their silent partner.

As far as the dance goes, however, I refuse to budge my position. I tell Jennifer to have fun at the Spring Fling and to show me pictures at school on Monday. She says she's going to call me from the dance to fill me in and give me the gossip. I'm sure she will.

I hang up and sit by the phone. Jennifer needs enough time to call Tanisha, explain that she failed, and for them to come up with a new tactic. The phone will ring again any minute. Even though I have stuff to do around the shop, I might as well stay where I am.

The phone rings.

"Hi Tanisha," I say, without checking the caller ID. "No thanks."

"Come on, Sylvie," she begs. "So what if things didn't work out with Adam? We totally respect your decision to break up. But you don't need a date to go to prom. You have us!"

"Nah," I tell Tanisha. And since we've been through this a thousand times already, she finally gives up. "I'll call with the reviews on the costumes in the morning," she says. I know I'll hear from her long before tomorrow. She'll call with Jennifer from the dance.

The afternoon wears on. I'm in the back of the store finishing up an invoice for some buttons when the front door chimes. I don't have any fitting appointments, so this must be a new customer. Dad ran out to pick up some tuxedos left at a hotel, so I'm in charge.

I come out from the back room saying, "Can I help you?"

"I hope so." It's Tyler.

That's strange. As far as I can recall, he's never been in the shop before.

"Hi," I say, stashing the invoice papers behind the front desk. "What's up?" I'm acting casual. The reality is that I'm not quite ready to tell him that I've thought about calling him, oh, say, about every five minutes, since I left the Corner Café yesterday afternoon. I'm trying to take control of my destiny, but it's way harder than I thought. Maybe tomorrow . . .

"What brings you to the shop?" I ask. "Did Cherise send you?"

"Cherise's at home," Tyler replies. "She's getting ready for the dance. Did you hear that Nathan's going to do AmeriCorps with her after graduation? Once Nathan gets finished at the UN, of course." He adds, "Mom and Dad weren't too happy at first, but after talking to Mrs. Feldman, they've mellowed. I think it's great. I hope they'll get placed in Manhattan."

"Yeah," I say. I know all that. Cherise told me because she's my best friend. Then again, she didn't fill me in about Nathan right away, so Tyler has reason to think she might be holding back information from me. All in all, this is a very weird conversation we're having.

"Do you want something?" I ask. Tyler's casually looking at some of the ties and cummerbunds we have on display. He picks up a purple cummerbund and holds it across his waist. With his black pants and T-shirt, the cummerbund completes his outfit.

"Purple?" I remark. "It's a big change."

"I like color," Tyler responds. "I think I've gone too long without any." He puts back the cummerbund and walks over to the desk. "Maybe I'll get some new white socks. I wouldn't want to make too many changes at once."

"Yeah," I say. "I can totally relate."

In the past month I've had a boyfriend, lost a boyfriend, gained two new friends, changed colleges, reconciled with my father, and accepted that my best friend's a pretty good astrologer. And I'm not quite done. There's one more change I'd like to make. If only I wasn't such a coward.

"Remember the big band gig that my manager got us for tonight?" Tyler props his elbows on the desk and leans in toward me. His breath smells like coffee. Black. Nice.

There's a rock of anticipation lodged in my belly.

"I figured we'd be jammin' at a club, but we aren't," he tells me.

"Where are you playing?" I ask. Since

neither of us are going to the prom, maybe he's going to invite me to another one of his gigs. That would be great. If I ever got my nerve up, I was going to ask him out, but this works even better.

"We're actually playing the Spring Fling Prom," Tyler says and my bubble of expectation immediately bursts.

"You are?" So much for him asking me on a date tonight. The ball's back in my court. I'm going to have to find the guts to ask him out another evening. "I'm surprised," I tell him. "Your band seems entirely antiprom to me."

"The original band cancelled because the bass player broke his thumb. The prom committee's paying us a lot," he says, looking down at the floor with squinted eyes. "It was a deal our manager couldn't refuse."

In the back of my head I hear a little voice telling me that now's my chance to go for it. Ask him out for next weekend. Tell him you're interested. Do something. Anything.

Drat. I'm a gutless wonder. I promise myself that I'll "go for it" next time. Maybe I'll take a trip to the roof tonight, look up at the stars, and find that boost in courage Tyler told me about. For now, I ask, "So, do you need a tuxedo? Is that why you're here?"

Tyler doesn't answer right away. Something on the floor's attracted his attention.

Suddenly, he disappears from view. I rise up on my tiptoes and peer over the counter top. Tyler's on his hands and knees, running his fingertips over a floorboard.

"Everything okay?" I ask.

"Sure," he replies. "I saw something glitter near my foot." And just like that, Tyler stands up, comes around the counter to where I am, and opens his hand. There it is, sitting in the center of his palm. . . .

My mother's lost diamond.

The old Sylvie didn't want a romance. She didn't want to date. Then, even when she had a boyfriend, the old Sylvie never made the first move. And the old Sylvie definitely didn't want to fall in love.

I'm not that old Sylvie anymore.

Next time is now. I don't need to look at the stars tonight. I'm a woman who is going to make her own destiny! Starting this very second.

I desperately want to kiss Tyler.

So I do.

And it's magic.

Twenty-four

Behind every frog is a handsome prince.
www.astrology4stars.com

"That was . . . ," Tyler stalls, searching for the right word. "Unexpected."

Yikes, that's not exactly what a girl wants to hear after she's made the first move.

Tyler pulls away from me and runs his hand through his hair.

"I . . . ," I begin to apologize for jumping him like that. "I didn't mean to . . . ," My words peter out as I place the diamond safely in the cash register and close the drawer.

"Finally!" Tyler exclaims, and then, this time, he does the jumping.

Our kiss is perfect. This is how kisses should be! Not too rushed or too slow. Just the right amount of pressure. He gives a little, I accept. I move closer, he encourages it. The room feels like it's spinning. Or perhaps time has stopped altogether. If this was a movie, there definitely would be fireworks bursting above the tuxedo shop.

"Wow," Tyler says, when at last he steps away. "Unexpected," he repeats, and this time I understand. Not that the kiss itself was unexpected, but rather the response that we both shared was a complete surprise. "Unexpected" turns out to be a compliment, not an insult.

We kiss again.

I don't hear the doorbell chime when Cherise comes rushing in. "I came over as soon as I realized. . . ." She's decked out in her doctor's costume for the dance and waving my astrological chart in the air.

"Whoa!" She blushes. "I can see that Tyler got here first."

"Realized what?" I'm a little embarrassed that Cherise just caught me liplocked with her brother. I try to step out of Tyler's embrace but he won't let me go. And I'm actually glad he won't.

"The stars!" Cherise explains why she's come bursting into the shop. "Turns out Madame Jakarta was right. I'm sorry I ever called her a quack." She strides over to the counter and lays out my star chart. "Madame Jakarta told me to rethink my predictions and in light of all that has happened, I did."

"Ever since you told me you'd broken up with Adam, I've been poring over your chart." She whips a brand-new Torah pointer out of her purse (Nathan bought her one of her very own) and stabs the chart with it. "When I made my initial prediction, Mars had entered Gemini. Gemini is the sign of twins." She glances up at Tyler with a wink. "Every step of the way, I thought the stars were pointing to Adam, but I was wrong. Jupiter, Scorpio, Aquarius, even Mercury, were all indicating a different love. The love of a twin! My twin!" She slaps herself on the forehead. "I can't believe I didn't see this coming before now."

"Cherise." Tyler says his sister's name with a tone I've never heard before.

"Yes?" she replied.

"Go away." Tyler glares at her and points at the shop door.

Cherise begins to protest, but then, after Tyler gives her a long, sinister look, she snatches up her chart and heads out. "See you tonight," she tells us, disappearing through the door as quickly as she entered.

"Cherise has a way of ruining a moment," Tyler says with a laugh. "Truth is, I came here to ask you to the prom. I've wanted to ask you for a while, but then the whole Cherise-astrology-Adam thing happened and I thought I lost my chance."

I look at him with squinted eyes as things begin to jell. "It was Wednesday when I found you standing by my locker. I was glad for the coincidence and gave you Cherise's skirt. It wasn't a coincidence, was it?" He shakes his head. "Were you planning to ask me out?"

"Kind of." Tyler half shrugs.

I immediately recall him asking if I wanted to go to the Corner Café after school. I didn't realize he meant without Cherise. It's all becoming clearer. "You *did* ask me out, didn't you?" When Cherise told me that some guy was going to ask me out, I never imagined it might be Tyler. I assumed that Adam was the one she meant. We both did. "I'm completely thickheaded," I tell him.

"You're not," he assures me. "I wasn't very clear then. But I plan to be now. Will you go with me to the prom? I know I'm playing with the band, but there will be breaks between the sets and we could have dinner first, then go to the after-party at Tanisha's, if you want. I know you like her and—"

"I can't," I interrupt. As much as I want to go out with him, tonight's prom is impossible.

Tyler looks crushed. "Do you have other plans?"

"No," I tell him. "It's just that I didn't expect to go. I never finished my costume."

"Oh." Tyler's face lights up. "Is that the only thing holding you back?"

"I suppose so."

"Problem solved," Tyler tells me, then pulls out his cell phone. I have no clue who he's calling, but what I hear him say is, "She said yes."

"No I didn't," I call out to the mystery person on the other end of the call.

Tyler snaps his phone shut. "You said that if you'd finished the costume, you'd go."

"I didn't say that," I pause. Grinning, I add, "Though I suppose it's true."

"Good," Tyler says, looking out the front door of the tux shop. "Now you can go with me."

In walks my father. Wanda's with him.

"My horoscope today said 'Tonight's the night for second chances.'" Tyler smiles. "Okay, so I didn't really read my horoscope, but that's what I imagine it would have said." He goes on, "I got up early, determined not to let opportunity slip by me again. So, I called for backup troops." He informs me that he didn't tell Cherise what he was up to, because she might blab. "Besides, she locked herself in her room this morning to review your natal chart." He stops for a second. "Or was it the lunar one?"

I cannot stop smiling. "Natal charts are more accurate," I tell him with a smile.

Turning, I face Tyler's "troops."

My father's standing in a stream of afternoon sunlight. There's a hanger in his hand. I look closer. He's holding the Cinderella dress out toward me. The multicolor patchwork of fabrics shimmer in the sun's sinking rays.

Now finished, the dress doesn't do justice to Tanisha and Jennifer's design. No. It is far more beautiful than even they could have imagined.

Without a word, Dad hands me the dress. I take it from him, sliding the fine materials through my fingers. It's amazing. Vera Wang herself couldn't have made a more perfect gown.

"When Tyler called, Wanda and I were more than happy to help out," Dad tells me. "Put it on, Sylvie."

"What about the tuxedos left at the hotel?" As I ask, it dawns on me that my father wasn't really out collecting tuxedos. He and Wanda must have been sewing all afternoon.

"A little white lie." My father takes a box from Wanda and gives it to me. "Wanda sewed while I ran a quick errand." The box feels heavy in my hands. Slowly, filled with anticipation, I lift the lid.

Clear plastic slippers. The modern equivalent of glass.

A tear rolls down my cheek. But this tear's an entirely different kind than the tears I shared last night with my dad. The tear that's falling now is not born of confusion. It's made of pure joy, appreciation, and true love.

I stretch up and kiss my dad on the cheek. Then I take the dress and hustle into the back room to try it on. The dress fits. The shoes, too. I haven't a clue where my father found faux glass slippers in Cincinnati, but they're just my size. As if they were created specially for my feet.

Dad brought the tiara I'd bought at the costume shop with him. I place it on my head and I'm ready.

I walk out of the back room, feeling more beautiful than ever. I might not have makeup on and I don't have a comb to run through my hair, but in this gown, I know I glow.

Tyler is standing by the shop's register, exactly where I left him. He's wearing a tuxedo. Black jacket, black pants, and . . . oh well, black shirt with a black cummerbund and black bow tie. I must say though, he's not looking so much Darth Vader tonight as Bond, James Bond.

My father steps forward, offering his arm. I move into his embrace. There's no music, but he gracefully spins me across the floor all the same.

I rest my head on Dad's shoulder and think about Cherise's dancing prediction. "When Neptune's moon is high in the sky, a guy you love and who loves you will ask you to dance." I don't have to look through my telescope to know that one of Neptune's moons is way up there tonight. I've fulfilled Cherise's prediction. Who'd have guessed it would be by dancing with my father.

I'm passed from one partner to the next as my father slips my arm off his and onto Tyler's. I'm not in love with Tyler, but there sure is potential. Loads of potential.

Being a man of few words, my dad has just one for us. "Go," is all he says.

A car horn sounds outside. Jennifer and Jordan, Tanisha and Lee, and Cherise and Nathan have swung by in their limo to pick us up. Apparently, Tyler planned for us all to quadruple date.

I whisper to Tyler I'd rather go out just us.

He winks and tells me we have plenty of time for that. "We'll have many, many dates just for us. Dates here in Cincinnati, dates in Cleveland in the fall, dates in New York when you come to visit." I can hardly wait.

But tonight, we're going to the Spring Fling Prom. We're going to dance until our feet hurt. And kiss until we're breathless.

Twenty-five

You have won the romance lottery.
Rejoice in your good fortune.
The stars are twinkling just for you.
Go out there and shine.
www.astrology4stars.com

I know what you're thinking. You're wondering if the diamond falling out of my mother's engagement ring really might have been a sign that love was headed my way.

Maybe Cherise's prediction was never meant to be about me and Adam. Perhaps, all along, it was supposed to be Tyler who was written in the stars.

Or maybe not.

It doesn't matter.

From here on out, Tyler and me, well, we're forging our own destiny.

And it's going to be perfect.

About the Authors

Stacia Deutsch and Rhody Cohon are the coauthors of the award-winning Blast to the Past chapter book series. Together, they have also ghostwritten for a mystery series and published two nonfiction texts. *In the Stars* is their first romantic comedy. Stacia wrote adult fiction before Rhody convinced her that they should work together and write children's literature instead. Stacia is married with three children and lives in Irvine, California. Rhody and her three children live in Tucson, Arizona.

★

My mother always tells me not to bite off more than I can chew.

"You run yourself ragged, Laine," she says. "You've got too much on your plate."

She's wrong.

I've got an appetite for achievement, fine. That much I'll give her. But these days, that's par for the course. I mean, college applications are up by, like, a million percent. It's a cutthroat competition. Where it used to be that your GPA and test scores were the most important aspect of your candidacy, now they're just the appetizer, or a playful sort of *amuse bouche*. You've got to bust your butt on extracurricular activities, and knock it out of the park with your interview and essay questions. And if you happen to score well on an AP exam or two? Well, that's merely the icing on the cake.

If I sound like a girl obsessed, there's a

reason. My parents split when I was little, and when it comes to tuition, it's really just Mom and me footing the bill. And while my mother's got a great job as chief restaurant critic for the *Philadelphia Tribune*, we're not exactly millionaires. I need to qualify for financial aid if I'm going to go somewhere other than Penn State.

Talk about type A, right? A junior in high school, and my cups—and my transcripts—already runneth over. Between advanced placement courses, SAT prep, extracurricular activities, and part-time jobs, I don't have a lot of free time. But, you know—if you can't stand the heat, get out of the kitchen.

I can stand the heat. Trust me, my life sometimes feels like one major pressure-cooker.

My mom would love it if I spent this summer at the pool club with my best friend, Anna, who's working as an au pair for a Cabana Club couple, flirting with boys and lazing in a lounge chair. That's what I did the past three summers, despite being highly allergic to sun. Anna and I had a good time—no, make that a *great* time—but times have changed.

When it comes to boys, I guess I have sort of a love-'em-and-leave-'em reputation. I can't help it: I see a cute guy and I immediately go all mushy. It's a disease. But now that we're revving up for senior year, it's time to get serious. I mean, I'm way too busy to let a guy distract me. No matter how yummy he is. I mean, I do date, but it's never anything serious. I reserve my seriousness for college planning, and all things related. Crushes are just a tasty little candy bowl to dip into when I'm running low on spice in my life. Or, to mix metaphors, if my life is a giant sugar cookie, then crushes are the rainbow sprinkles on top. If life is like a pizza, then crushes are the pepperoni topping. If life is . . . a cheeseburger, than crushes are a side of fries.

You get the point. I may like my French fries (and I do), but they're never going to take the place of a solid main course.

I know some girls think I have my priorities mixed up. And I've been called a tease by some of the boys I've dated, boys who wanted to be more than a side dish in the menu of my life. But college isn't just a pie-in-the-sky fantasy, and as I'm constantly reminding Anna, too many cooks spoil the broth.

My life, my broth. Boys will have to be back-burnered. . . .

For now.

Charm your way to the top with this tongue-in-chic guide.

THE
SOCIAL
CLIMBER'S
GUIDE
TO
HIGH
SCHOOL

a tongue-in-chic handbook by
robyn schneider

THE SOCIAL CLIMBER'S GUIDE TO HIGH SCHOOL
Robyn Schneider

It takes serious social-climbing skills to reach the peak
of the A-list now—making varsity cheerleading isn't
even a start. This hip handbook will help you step
behind the velvet rope of high school popularity. After
all, so what if you weren't invited to last weekend's
hottest party? You can always read about it on
someone's blog and pretend you were there. . . .

Nonboring, Nonpreachy: Nonfiction

From **Simon Pulse**

Published by Simon & Schuster

Get smitten with these sweet & sassy British treats:

Prada Princesses
by Jasmine Oliver

Three friends tackle the high-stakes world of fashion school.

10 Ways to Cope with Boys
by Caroline Plaisted

What every girl *really* needs to know.

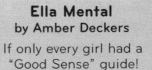

Ella Mental
by Amber Deckers

If only every girl had a "Good Sense" guide!